BILLY FIDGET'S
FAMILY FORTUNES

Nick Battle and Eric Delve

BILLY FIDGET'S
FAMILY FORTUNES

The continuing adventures of Billy Fidget

HODDER

First published in Great Britain in 2013 by Hodder & Stoughton
An Hachette UK company

This paperback edition first published in 2014
1

A CIP catalogue record for this title is available from the British Library

ISBN 978 1 444 70364 1
eBook ISBN 978 1 444 70363 4

Typeset in Scala by Hewer Text UK Ltd, Edinburgh

Printed and bound in the UK by Clays Ltd, St Ives plc

Hodder & Stoughton policy is to use papers that are natural, renewable
and recyclable products and made from wood grown in sustainable
forests. The logging and manufacturing processes are expected to
conform to the environmental regulations of the country of origin.

Hodder & Stoughton Ltd
338 Euston Road
London NW1 3BH

www.hodderfaith.com

For my wife Nicky,
my daughters Misha and Jodie and my son Jesse.
Nick Battle

For my wife Pat,
our daughters Sarah, Joanne and Rebekah,
our sons Glenn and Andy,
their partners and our wonderful grandchildren.
Eric Delve

PROLOGUE

MARCH 31st

Dear God,

What a glorious day! You should have been there. I'm sorry, I'm forgetting – of course, you were! Wasn't it fantastic? I have never seen Helen looking more radiant, her auburn hair swept off her face and wearing a gorgeous ivory dress. The fragrance that was in the air. The sweetest scent I've ever inhaled. Not sweet in a cloying sense – but it kind of wraps itself around you and leaves you feeling light, warm and peaceful. All at the same time.

And the children, well, they were amazing too. All three of them grinning from ear to ear as they followed Helen down the aisle of the church. Tom and Jack bedecked in charcoal grey suits, crisp white linen shirts and deep burgundy ties and Annabel looking just like a beautiful and petite version of her mum, with her matching ivory dress and burgundy pashmina. Did you like the music? I know that 'One Moment in Time' by Whitney Houston is not your typical hymn but I hope you enjoyed it – we did.

It was a sacred day, because I know what happens when the vow breaks. I can't believe how bad things were just a few months ago. And I remember when I married Helen back in the day. I never gave the *vows* much thought. But after all we've been through . . . well actually after all I put my family through, it was incredible to be given a second chance like that. But that's the business you're in isn't it? Rescuing losers like me, people at the last chance saloon. And that's where I was. No getting away from it. Still, no looking back, eh God? Well maybe occasionally just to remind myself of just how blessed I am, if you know what I mean. Oh by the way – Tom said he'll be in touch soon . . . actually I should tell you he got more than a little carried away on our big day; he and his mate trying everyone's drinks and cigarettes – they ended up very much the worse for wear. Kids eh? Jack wants to know if he'll get 'Woody' from *Toy Story* for Christmas. Helen sends her love of course and Annabel says, 'Hi.'

Love from your son,

Billy

PS We decided to repeat our original vows – word for word. I REALLY held it together even with the 'Forsaking all others – 'til death us do part.' I am SO grateful. Thank you.

APRIL 1st

Billy, my son,

Congratulations! And very well done. You came through all kinds of difficult tests to arrive at this moment of triumph. Today has been a pinnacle day for you. Of course I was there. And yes it was truly glorious. As you came close to me, the glory that surrounds me wrapped itself around you two. That's why everything had that extra shine. The whole day was permeated with radiance – and the fragrance? Same thing! The scent of heaven. Just as I am closer than breathing, heaven is always close, but is hidden from your world. In your love for each other and for me, you and Helen created what an ancient people called 'A thin place'. The veil between heaven and earth became porous. Treasure this day, because other days will come when life will be much more difficult. Moments like this, mountain peaks of joy and glory, are days to be treasured, days to be held firmly in your memory banks, so that when darker days come you can remind yourself that though it may feel all-surrounding, the darkness is not the only truth. In the end it cannot win.

You mentioned the song 'One Moment in Time'. I love that song. It represents the longing of human beings, as they cry out to me for what they instinctively know inside them is true. They have a destiny, a dream for which they were made. The yearning for that dream is what makes people human. When it dies, something in their humanity dies as well. By the way, who are you kidding? *'I REALLY held it together on "Forsaking all others – 'til death us do part."'* Everybody there, not just me, knew you were struggling. Why didn't you let go? If a man cannot weep with joy at such a moment, it is a crying shame . . . So hold the picture in your mind, especially the picture of the children. This isn't just a new day for you and Helen, but for them too. *Don't be afraid to be vulnerable.*

Here's my promise – no matter what happens to them and how far away from me at times they may walk, I will never abandon them. I will follow them, love them and always draw them back to me.

Your proud and ever-loving Father,

GOD

APRIL 4th

Dear God,

Great to hear from you and have your promise to look out for the kids. I loved that idea of 'a thin place', like somehow the space between heaven and earth is just like tissue paper. I think music can take me there more easily than anything else. Like a guitar solo that transports you and lifts you up and leaves you feeling better than before, or the way Eva Cassidy used to sing – breathtaking and beautiful. 'I wish I knew you like this as a child ah . . .' but what do they say? 'Youth is wasted on the young.' Well it certainly was for me. Still, we're all older and hopefully wiser now. I'm so looking forward to our second honeymoon. Helen and I have rented a villa not far from Nice in the south of France. I'll send you a postcard!

Love you God,

Billy x

PS There is something very wonderful about an older woman. I mean Helen. All that experience. Admittedly the chassis may not be as buffed and polished as it used to be (but neither is mine).

BILLY FIDGET'S FAMILY FORTUNES

FIVE YEARS LATER

MAY 4th

Hello Billy,

Long time, no speak.

Just wanted to ask, 'How's the love life?' I remember you saying a few years back, 'When I make love to Helen now, it's better than anything I've experienced before.' Or something along those lines. Maybe you described it more in 'old' Billy's vernacular. In any event I hope you are delighting in the gift I gave you both for each other. The Romans used to say, 'After sex a man is sad.' Thousands of years ago they discovered it – using and abusing people makes you lonelier, sadder and angrier. Real love-making draws you into a circle of love and mutual pleasure. It can at times be like your experience of music. It becomes 'a thin place' – your pleasure mirrors the pleasure of heaven. That power and purity is divine. The moment when heaven and earth intersect is what every addict is looking for, dreaming of in the next fix. The same longing drives every sex addict – 'perhaps next time!' Every drunk is looking for it in the next bottle. They are looking in the wrong places. But at least they're looking, and, in the final analysis, looking for me. That is why, believe it or not, there is hope for them.

Look out for your son Tom ... he is just entering the phase of life when enchanting idealism and rampant stupidity march hand in hand. Keep praying, Billy. You're going to need loving patience as well as strong and tender discipline. It's a good job you have me as your Father! By the way, don't be too hard on the lad. He is after all 50% your DNA!

Bless you my son.

Always your loving Dad,

GOD

MAY 22nd

Dear God,

I've taken the family away to Spain for half term. What with Tom about to take his A levels it might be the last chance we get to go away all together. I'm sat by the pool, the sun is shining, Annabel and Jack are splashing around. Tom is a few yards away laid comatose on a lounger with his headphones glued to his ears. Reading Milton's *Paradise Lost*. How he can do the two things together I just don't know.

Helen is asleep in bed today – says she's not feeling too well so I thought I'd take a few moments to write back. Thanks for the advice. That's really helpful and as usual *so* insightful. Particularly from you. I mean have you ever ... you know? What I mean to say is just how can you be such an expert on the subject when a) you're not married and b) you're not over the side with someone else's wife? Just another of your great mysteries is it? Sent to baffle me and drive me bonkers ... you know what I mean. You're right about the whole addiction thing. I was addicted to sex – I just hope that I haven't passed that rogue gene from my side of the family on to Tom in his DNA. So many of his peers at school seem to be exploring all that life has to offer, sexually and chemically. I know it's important that everybody should get to feel immortal for a short time in their life. You know: that feeling that the world is your oyster and anything can happen! Anything is possible! We can change the world!

Sadly that seems to dissipate all too quickly; innocence is eroded faster than a tsunami engulfing a coastal town. Some of Tom's friends just turned sixteen and they're already world weary. Burnt out from diving into a dark and deep moral abyss. Tragic really. Anyway got to run now – I think I can hear Helen being sick in the bathroom . . . Write soon please.

Love,

Billy

MAY 23rd

Dear Billy,

I love the sense of pleasure with which you write about the simple joys of your holiday. So few people understand what David the poet wrote to me: *'God – I know I'm on the right track with you. When I hang out with you there is real life and overflowing joy – pleasures forever.'*

Now that was what surprised you when you first made my acquaintance. Sadly, in your culture I seem to have a reputation as a cosmic killjoy. (It's not only politicians who suffer from bad press.) Hopefully, in my case, you might like to consider that the bad press is wholly unjustified! I am glad you enjoyed what I said. I really do chuckle when you struggle to ask me simple questions like 'Hello God, have you ever had sex?' to which I could only ask you, 'Have you ever had sex? Truly?' You know what it is? It's the expression in your human bodies of total loving commitment between two people who are completely given to each other in every fibre of their being. We gave it to you, a present, a gift from us – Father, Son and Holy Spirit. So that you would have just a little bit of insight into the love we have and the joy we know with each other. This is the very heartbeat of heaven itself. So, if you see it from our perspective, it's not such a mystery that we understand sex. The real mystery is that you understand it so little. We crafted it as our special gift to you, to Helen and every member of the human race. Its dynamic, its power was programmed to draw men and women out of

13

the selfishness of their own needs, to actually give themselves, not just their bodies, but themselves. Perhaps that explains why your addiction to sex never satisfied the longing deep inside.

Sadly, you're right about the generation in which Tom is growing up. Instead of choosing the adventure, they choose to exploit each other. It's consumerism. It robs them of all meaning and steals away their idealism. Consumerism makes cynics of them all before they've even had a chance to discover their dreams. Their ideals are seared out of them by the acid of relationships without love, emotions without connection, sex without commitment. Your concern about Tom's friends is well placed. Keep praying for him. The best you can do for him is to provide a kind of spiritual force field around him. Your prayers, connected with my love, and faith that refuses to surrender him to the darkness in spite of whatever stupidity he may display – these things will win through in the end. Give Helen a cuddle and remind her I'm her Dad and am very proud of her. A surprise is coming and you are going to need more of my grace. Remember I still am your immensely proud Father in heaven.

Love,

GOD

MAY 24th

Dear God,

About the surprise . . . I know what it is. I woke up this morning to find a pregnancy test kit laid on the pillow where Helen's head would normally be. Two. Blue. Lines. I am completely freaked out. And she says she thinks she must be four months already; she thought if her periods were stopping it was early menopause and that I certainly wouldn't cope with that. But I've got to tell you, this is worse! We've got three children already! Why do we need any more? Oh yes, it's nice to know my guys are still swimming, I'll be honest that part positively makes me glow with pride. But by the time the child is twenty I will be *seventy!* I'll probably never see him or her get married and I will certainly never see their children. And then there are the financial consequences. I don't have a pension, money has always been so sporadic, and it was going to be hard enough surviving as we were, without an extra mouth to feed in our old age! I don't know how to tell Helen but I simply do not want another child. Our family is complete, thank you very much. What do you think you're playing at? Anyway I'm going now – I can hear her coming up the stairs. You'd better come up with something pretty good, I can feel my chest tightening, my wallet constricting and I can't begin to tell you what's happening down below!

Love,

Billy

MAY 24th

Hi God,

   It's me, Helen – I've had a bit of a shock. Life has been really good these last five years, since we retook our vows, the kids are for the most part all doing fine, and Billy well . . . he's been like a young man in his twenties rather than somebody in middle age. I always thought men were at their peak at twenty but Billy . . . well, frankly, he's been insatiable. The thing is – you and I already know I'm pregnant but for Billy, I think it will come as a rather traumatic shock. You certainly are the God of surprises! Anyway, can you please watch over us as I've left the test kit on my pillow and I'm just about to take him his morning cuppa. Black coffee. No sugar. I think he'll be needing it. Thanks, God – I feel at this stage in life that this new baby is a gift. I don't know about our Billy though.

   Love,

   Helen x

MAY 25th

Dear Helen,

Thanks for yours. Yes, I realise it is a bit of a shock to you. As for Billy, he has been experiencing for the first time in his life what it is to actually make love. Before, it was always a mechanical desire to satisfy a kind of inner itch. Now he has discovered the longing to be truly one with the one that he loves and that is the best aphrodisiac there is.

I am glad you are pleased about the baby. Keep rejoicing because your pleasure will spill over and begin to change Billy. You're wise – you already know intuitively that this news will leave him staggering. In fact, he'll be truly fearful. But he will eventually learn to trust if he sees that joy and peace in you. If he gets grumpy – and he will – don't let that rob you of your joy. It may well feel that he is blaming you, but it's just his fear talking. He has to work through that. Simply fix your gaze on me; let my peace flood you and, without saying a word, you will be to him a sign of peace. It will take a while to get through. But he'll get it in the end.

Thank you for discerning that, particularly this stage in life, this one is a gift, a special child, a child of your love. I am so proud of you and rejoice along with you.

Always your loving Dad,

GOD

MAY 25th

Billy, my dear son,

What are you panicking about? I thought we had been through all of this stuff about fear. But, OK, that was fear in a different area of life. Fear about personal safety, physical danger and the lives of your family. So let's get this straight. I'm the God who says *Fear not* in *every* situation and circumstance. I'm bigger – always bigger! No matter what the problem may be, whatever difficulty you face, I am still Lord of the whole universe. And when it comes to fathering a child at your age, why shouldn't you feel a certain measure of joy and pride? I hear your anxiety as you say, 'By the time the child is twenty, I will be seventy years old!' What are you saying? When you are seventy, you are as good as dead? Ask your friends who are seventy – they will tell you to get lost! It's certainly possible to sparkle with life, laughter and energy at that age as much as at yours.

Where does this stuff come from that tells you that you will probably never see this child get married and, even worse, 'certainly' never see their children – how do you know that? I am the one who knows the future and I haven't told you anything remotely like that. Oh, right – I see. Your mum died early so you must be going to as well. Never accept that kind of programming in your thinking, Billy. I, the Eternal God, am your Father. When you die is in my hands. I have far better plans for you than the pronouncements you've made over yourself. So here's what I want you to do. It's very simple – repent! Take back what you wrote to me. Take back the thought. *I* am the one in whom your future rests. I'm the one who has promised that I will give you energy to the very end of your days. I am also the one who has promised that if you walk with me, I will make your life long and satisfying.

As for the financial consequences, when you look back, can't you see? Even when you were running away from me, I still watched over you. Even when you were absolutely blind in your rebellion, somehow your needs were met. Why assume that I will abandon you now? Again we go back to your childhood – the Billy that was abandoned and so often let down by his earthly father needs to learn that his heavenly Father will never abandon him or fail him. Here is my promise: 'I will never let you down, never walk away and leave you – NEVER!'

How do you tell Helen about the way you feel? Be honest. But don't leave me out of the equation. Tell her you're frightened. But tell her you trust me to get you through. And be at rest. Let your heart feel my peace and your chest relax. Your wallet should be informed that I have promised to provide! And may the nether regions of your body truly know peace!

Always your loving and proud,

Father GOD

PS Don't dismiss this child – genuinely a love child. So give your fear to me, and rejoice. Remember, it's not just about you and me. You are a part of the body of Jesus on earth. Other people love you and are there for you. Don't be too scared to contact them.

MAY 25th

From: Billy
To: Haakon
! HIGH IMPORTANCE

Dear Haakon,

I know it's a while since we've been in touch and I'm sorry about that. But you prayed for me for over twenty years and you learnt to love me. I'm writing to you because you are the nearest thing I've got to an earthly dad. I don't know whether you've heard, but Helen is pregnant with our fourth child. All I can think is, I'm fifty and I will be seventy by the time the child is twenty. I'm not even sure I will live that long. Heavenly Father keeps telling me to trust him. He says I should let my heart feel his peace. But right at the moment, all I can feel is a kind of great big scream building up inside like an express train just about to burst out of me. I am in a total state of panic and although God keeps saying trust him, I just don't know how. Why am I in such a panic? Why am I so scared? It's just a baby, for God's sake! You once called yourself my father in God. Well, please be a dad to me now. Tell me, what am I supposed to do?

Your son in God (I hope),

Billy

MAY 26th

From: Haakon
To: Billy
! High Importance

Billy, my dear son in God,

There's no need for there to be any question about it. That is what you are, my son in God. I think even in eternity, that relationship will still be there. There's more to being a father than just the process of conception. I have become your true dad and I'm proud to be. Don't doubt it.

What are you going to do with that fear inside you? The only advice I can give you is this. If there's a scream inside, then let it out. Scream at God. He's not going to be shocked. He knows the fear that's buried deep inside. Give it to him. Don't stay with the fear. Let it go. Scream it out; let God have it then begin to allow his peace to be breathed over you. Remember you're not just my son. Far more importantly, you are his son and he loves you far, far more than I do. Will be in touch. I will give you a phone call soon.

Always,

Haakon

MAY 26th

Dear God,

OK, so my mother's death has haunted me. She left this earth far too early and in a horribly painful manner. At times like this all I have left are my lifelong mantras: Life is short and then you die. Enjoy life while you can, it is not a rehearsal. Get them before they get you. Leave them before they leave you. If I'm on my own, no one can hurt me.

So no, I never expected to live a long time. To be honest I probably thought I'd be dead by my mid-twenties. But you had other plans. I know – and you're going to tell me again – that these mantras are wrong. But they are so ingrained in me – I'm going to need help to dislodge them, and frankly I'm not sure any more that I want to, not when you pull a trick like this.

So, yes, I'm sorry for being such an ungrateful bastard but I am human you know. Superbilly was just a figment of my youthful imagination.

Love,

Billy

PS I do worry about money; who doesn't, in the current economic climate? You say you'll provide and stuff but like they say, 'The Lord helps those who help themselves.' And no, I'm not talking about nicking stuff or doing one of my old dodgy deals. But it's good to be proactive, isn't it?

MAY 27th

Dear God

I know it's 2am, but I thought of something else. What if, when we do the scan, the baby's not healthy and we're advised to abort? What if it's born deformed? What am I supposed to do then? Let me know.

Thanks,

Billy

MAY 27th

My dear son,

You already know that nothing in your letter was a surprise to me. But I'm glad that at last you have faced these things and clearly stated what they are – poisonous lies that have wormed deep inside you. Look again at those statements. You most truthfully described them as *mantras*, texts of spiritual power used as an incantation, chanted or inwardly repeated in order to press words and their meanings deep into the human soul. So, these statements have become chains around your spirit. Why are they so powerful? Because you forged them on the anvil of your anger in response to the pain in your childhood: first, the abuse of your father, then the drawn-out agonised death of your mother. Suffering almost always generates anger, and a sense that these things should not be. The rage at what happened becomes outrage, a desire to find someone and blame them for it all. The wounded child inside says, 'I will hang on to the pain. The bitter nature of reality is now clear. It will define my view of life. I will NOT allow myself to believe otherwise. If there is anyone out there responsible for my hurt, I hope they are wounded by my unbelief and anger.'

You are not alone. Many people close themselves in with walls of bitterness. The truth is, that is where you would have stayed if it had not been for your fear of Eddie Fast. Now you know your analysis of life based on fear was deeply flawed. Real life is different. Healing is possible because Love is real. Grace is available. Hope is priceless and Faith works when empowered by Love. You have broken out of the prison. Your glib expectation of being dead by your mid-twenties has been completely thwarted. You are absolutely right – I did indeed have other plans. Aren't you glad?

Your loving Father,

GOD

MAY 27th

Hi God,

   That's all well and good but you haven't exactly answered my questions. Are you having an off day?
   Love,

   Billy

MAY 27th

Dear Billy,

No I'm not having an 'off day' but I did want to have your full attention.

Now let's look at these bitter affirmations of disappointment:

Life is short and then you die.

My old friend, David, had a different view. His childhood was filled with rejection and the pain of the early death of his mother. In spite of that, he kept the faith with determined courage, saying, 'My times are in your hand,' and don't forget, he killed Goliath with a catapult!

Enjoy life while you can, it is not a rehearsal.

My son Jesus declared his purpose like this: 'I came so they can have real and eternal life, more and better life than they ever dreamed of.' So, Billy, seize the day. Enjoy, my son! You don't need to be desperate. Just go with the flow of the life I've given you. But remember, this life *is* a rehearsal – for the life you will live with me in eternity.

Get them before they get you.

I couldn't agree more! My pal Solomon said, 'If your enemy is hungry, feed him. If he is thirsty, give him a drink. For in so doing you will heap coals of fire on his head.' Better to cover them with embarrassment because of your kindness than to launch a vendetta that could last for generations. Your brother Jesus added that we should actively try and bless those who are being horrible to us.

Leave them before they leave you.

Only one answer to that! Would you want me to treat you like that? My friend Paul's answer was, 'Love never gives up, never loses faith, is always hopeful and endures through everything.'

If I'm on my own, no one can hurt me.

Except, of course, YOU! If you're on your own, you are locked in a prison with yourself and people's capacity to wound themselves is astonishing. It is also true that if you're on your own, no one can love you, heal you or bind up your broken heart. That's why Jesus came, to enter the dark prison of loneliness with eternal friendship.

You called yourself *ungrateful*. Bear in mind there has never been anybody truly deeply miserable who at the same time was truly deeply grateful. Those two things just cannot co-exist. Gratitude enhances every pleasure and opens you up to grace – unexpected and undeserved good things that I send into your life from time to time. In truth, gratitude is the central plank of all true pleasure. It may seem strange but, for me, that is what defines human life – not ingratitude, but joyous access to grace through thankfulness. Think about it. If you engage with that long enough, maybe the true Superbilly will not be simply a figment of your youthful imagination! The best is always yet to be, you know.

Your loving Dad,

GOD

PS In our last series of letters, you said you would start to call me DAD but I notice you've pulled back from doing that – is there a reason?

28

MAY 28th

Dear God,

   How am I supposed to try and get my heart and head round that last letter you sent me? I'll have a go, but can't promise anything. As for calling you Dad, maybe you'll say it's moments like this when I need to, but that's just when I struggle most with it. I just don't think you get it. I'm rocked to my foundations.
   Sorry.

   Billy

MAY 28th

Billy,

I'm still the God who says 'Fear not in *every* situation and circumstance.' I'm always bigger than every possible circumstance. And my love for you continually grows. The prospect of this baby has really shaken you, hasn't it? It has exposed raw nerve-endings deep within you, creating a paralysing dread touching almost every area of life. This opens up your spirit to receive suggestions coming from the Prince of Fear himself.

Why suppose a scan will show the baby is not healthy and you will be advised to abort it? Your wife is, as they say, 'expecting'. It's a lovely word. Why not, together with her, expect a beautiful healthy baby who will be a golden child, reflecting the new love you've discovered between you, a child who will be the embodiment of the joy you now share?

The temptation to journey into the future in your mind, in order to worry about everything that might happen there is horribly addictive. The more you think about things that could go wrong, the more things you will discover. Trying to fix it all is never-ending. Don't you have enough trouble to deal with today? Get on with living. Deal with today's problems and you'll discover that I'm there, walking each step of the way with you.

Just suppose a scan shows an abnormality. And suppose health professionals advise an abortion. IF that happens you'll discover then that you have sufficient strength to deal with it and enough wisdom to work out the right course of action. I'm big enough to deal with it when that day comes. So, entrust the baby to me. If it were born deformed then I would expect you to follow my heart – to see beyond the deformity and love my image in your child.

Remember, anxiety never solves a problem. But it often creates a pathway for the feared thing on which it's focussed to move towards you.

The most powerful factor in human destiny is the invisible spiritual reality of the heavenly realm. Fear increases the odds that the thing most feared will happen. Fear is deadly. That is why in my book it says 'Fear not' 366 times. That covers every day of the year, even in a leap year!

As I've said before – your enemy is profoundly malicious and very cunning. He knows how to insert a thought into your mind so you think it's your idea. Discernment from my Spirit will help you choose the good and reject the bad.

When it comes to your question, *Who doesn't worry about money in the current economic climate?* the answer is, someone who trusts in me instead. Everybody else worries about it, especially the rich.

As for the old adage, 'The Lord helps those who help themselves,' that kind of folk wisdom – along with such delightful sayings as 'Someone's got to worry about it!' and 'Charity begins at home' – is all about fear. It produces constricted lives of increasing meanness and misery.

You asked about proactivity. Yes, it's good to be proactive, intentionally trusting in me and listening to my voice. So day by day you wind up walking with me step by step,

Father and son working together. That kind of proactivity produces joy, creativity and genuine security. It's definitely time to consign all that fear-based folklore to the dustbin and adopt as your mantra instead 'I will trust and not be afraid.' It's a good one and has served generations of my children very well. It builds an inner security that nothing can take away.

Bless you, my son. I am proud that you are wrestling with all this. Don't forget I'm truly the everlasting God and whatever you come up with, I am always bigger and my love for you is always stronger.

Your ever-loving and truly BIG,

Daddy

MAY 29th

Phone call

Haakon: *Hello, is that Billy?*

Billy: *Haakon, thank God! I'm so glad to hear your voice. Thanks for calling.*

Haakon: *So how are you doing?*

Billy: *Ah. Sorry, Haakon. Not very well. I try to let God's peace come in. But it's like there's a pressure inside me that won't let it penetrate. I don't even understand why I'm so afraid.*

Haakon: *Billy, I'm not an expert in these things. I wouldn't pretend to be. But I do know this has a lot to do with your family background, the death of your mother and your fear of being left alone.*

Billy: *So, what do I do?*

Haakon: *In all the years I've been walking with God, I have learnt just a few things. One is to trust him, not just with words, but with everything. For too many years I tried to hide what was in my heart. I was so ashamed. I just couldn't bring myself to expose to him what I'd done. Even when I did, I could tell no one. But over the years as I prayed for you, I learnt to forgive you, and Sara did too.*

Billy: *I know and I'm really grateful. I still can't believe it at times, but I know it's true.*

Haakon: *Right. So often that's the way we are with God's forgiveness. We know it's true, but we can't quite believe it. It's to do with not forgiving ourselves, but even more, not trusting him as Father. Your relationship with your biological dad left a bad legacy. You've come a long way, Billy. The* only thing I can say is give God the fear. Scream at him if you want to. Shout, swear at him. Release the anger and fear. Then let God breathe his peace over you. His grace is gigantic and he loves you far more than you know. You need to trust him with everything.

Billy: I know. Pray for me. Please.

Haakon: All the time.

Billy: No, I mean now.

Haakon: I know – just teasing. Loving Father, thank you for my beloved son, Billy. I have watched him grow in faith and grace. I've seen him respond with courage again and again to things that Satan has thrown at him. Now I pray. Give him all the courage he needs to release his fear and anger to you. Let him know more than ever before just how much you love him. Father, may he truly understand that you approve of him. You smile on him because you love him, even as I do. AMEN.

Billy: Thanks, Haakon. Thanks for the call. I won't forget it and I won't forget your prayer. Honest. With your help and his, I'll get through this. Thanks. Talk to you soon.

Haakon: Bye, Billy. Bless you, my son.

JUNE 1st

Dear God,

Well finally we're home. Leaving the pregnancy kit for Billy as a 'surprise', may not have been the smartest thing I've ever done. He tried hard to look pleased, but I could tell he was totally freaked out. He ended up sat in front of the television for the rest of the holiday drinking copious amounts of red wine and watching very violent and dark films and saying virtually nothing. It was like the old days – the days before he met you. Even now I would say that he's acting like he's completely depressed. I've tried to get him to see that this child is a gift, literally, from you. And as such we should be looking forward to what this new arrival will bring. But all Billy does is ask me if I know the statistics about how many children born to women over the age of forty have Downs Syndrome, and he follows that up with how he doesn't want to be a carer for the rest of his life and did I know that by the time he or she goes off to university he'll be seventy? Now I know that as the Bible puts it, 'All things work together for good' but as far as I can see, we seem to be wallowing in the mire as opposed to rolling in the hay! I'd be so grateful for your wisdom on this but also your advice on how to handle my husband. He's been a great dad since he met you and I know once the child is born he'll be great again. But how do we get him, if you'll excuse the pun, 'over the hump'?

Love,

Helen x

JUNE 2nd

Helen, dear daughter,

Truthfully, given the issue now welling up in Billy's life, there was no easy way of letting him know you were pregnant. He is facing the reality everyone who follows me must face. With their minds they want to do the right thing, but with their hearts they find themselves rebelling against it. He knows he should be pleased. But he is ambushed by his own history. It's not long since he turned to face the problems of his childhood. Those problems go very deep. After years of running away from his love for you and your love for him, he finally discovered how glorious it is to love one woman as I intended him to. To discover that that one woman loved him the same way, released in him a joy he had never known before.

Because he's changed he's finding this a struggle. Before, when you were pregnant, he was running into the arms of other women. He never faced the issue. Now he faces the fact that someone new is coming on the scene – someone who threatens his place in your heart, and even in mine. It's not rational. He knows it doesn't make sense. But then fear never does. It's the terror of his childhood.

Booze has always been one of his escapes and violent films are like a drug too, feeding the habit of hopelessness. Yes, he is depressed and even more so because he knows what you've said – the child is a gift from me – and he is afraid because of it. His anxieties are completely illogical and contradictory.

It's all about his fear of abandonment, of being rejected. Feeling alone. When you say 'All things work together for good,' that is true. You might find it helpful to take it more personally. I say to you and Billy: 'In every situation, I work things together for your good.' What is happening is going to set him free, believe it or not. True, Billy is wallowing – don't join him! Love him faithfully and tenderly. But don't indulge his self-pity. He has to come through it and he will. How do we get him 'over the hump'? Actually, he's the one that's got the hump! And he'll have to get over it himself. But we will love him and support him through it. I am especially proud of you for the way you are dealing with this. Just don't let Billy's misery get you down. Take time to be with me and let my smile rest upon you.

Always and forever,

Your loving Dad

JUNE 8th

Dear God,

Thank you so much for writing – your wisdom and insight is so very helpful. To give Billy his due, we sat down the other night and talked into the early hours ... He made sense at first but once he'd opened the second bottle of wine (bet he didn't tell you about that, did he?) he started to ramble a bit. I think we got somewhere though and he at least feels he's been listened to ... beneath all of Billy's bluster I think he's secretly chuffed that a man of his age can still, as he put it, 'fire on all cylinders'. He watches way too much Top Gear! Anyway, I think our chat about his health and seeing the baby grow up worked. He has at least agreed to cut back on his wine a bit. If only our Tom could do the same. I'm getting quite worried about whatever it is that keeps him out to three o'clock in the morning. He's so tired and spaced out ... but I guess it's partly in his DNA – plus he sees it in his dad, what the psychologists would call 'learned behaviour'. Please continue to watch over us. My life ... OUR life, is so much better in relationship with you. But it is still a rocky road and I don't know what I'd do without you.

Love,

Helen xxx

JUNE 10th

Helen, my dear daughter,

It's always good to hear from you. You're right – Billy did well to sit down and speak out the stuff he's been feeling but not truly recognising. Of course he didn't mention the second bottle of wine. But then, as you know, I knew already. And he knows that. When it comes to his feeling secretly chuffed, of course you're right again. You've seen him at those odd moments when he's passing a mirror and pulls in his stomach, gives himself the thumbs up and smiles. Oh yes, I think he's quite proud of himself. He will be imagining himself showing the baby to his friends with a certain modest pride. That's why you were so wise to talk to him about the baby growing up and him being there. You've given him the motivation he needs. And I will always strengthen him.

Tom is at a crucial stage. He's in the grip of peer pressure from friends who are not truly friends. The leader of the group certainly shows some self-destructive patterns of behaviour. But don't forget Tom has more than just his earthly dad's DNA. He has my spiritual DNA and, believe it – my DNA trumps Billy's DNA every time! He hasn't yet discovered it, but Tom has a gift of leadership. The behaviour he learned from watching his dad and the spiritual inheritance that came with that is nowhere near as powerful as my grace. I am never going to let go of him. And then of course he's seen how his dad has changed. You ask me to watch over the family. Always. Just as I loved you from the moment you were born and also Billy, so I have loved each of your children since before they were conceived. My plans for them are bigger than anything you could dream of. So never pray prayers of despair. Always pray believing for the best, because that's Tom's inheritance. When Billy and then you committed your lives to me, and opened yourselves up to my presence, you created for your children a new inheritance, a heavenly one, a purpose and destiny that can never be stolen from them, though they may of course turn away from it. Even then, though, my love will never leave them. So no matter what may happen, trust them to me and be at peace.

Sleep well dear girl.

Your loving Dad,

GOD

JUNE 11th

Dear God,

I'm feeling a lot better about everything. It's all going to be all right. Right?

Love,

Billy

JUNE 13th

Dear Billy,

How long have you known me now? Please trust me.
Love, as ever,

Dad

JUNE 18th

Dear God,

Maybe I was wrong about saying it was going to be all right – feeling all unsure again. I just didn't expect to find myself here. With my kids growing up faster than I'd like, and me having just celebrated my fiftieth birthday and now I'm about to be a dad again . . . I mean, after all we as a family have been through – it's a bit rich! But then life will never be dull, right? And I would never want it to be. But this just feels like a huge stretch for me.

And when I get stressed, well, I hit the default 'old' Billy button. I know that's not the way to go about life – but as I see it you're still moulding me. The potter and the clay and all that. By the way, Helen's already complaining of feeling tired and we're not even at the three-month mark yet. She says she thinks we should tell the children soon as they'll guess otherwise. That is if they haven't done so already. Pretty smart bunch as you know. By the way, thinking of embarking on a new career – felt a bit stuck in a rut with the whole car sales thing. Any ideas welcomed!

Love,

Billy

PS About not calling you Dad. Sorry about that. I was sulking!

JUNE 19th

Hello my son,

I always love it when you are honest about your grumpiness. I really cannot be doing with the sort of people who tell me what they think I want to hear, politely lying through their teeth. So, your wife is pregnant again. What did you expect? You have rediscovered sex. And now you have rediscovered that sex produces children. Well now, there's a shock! And yes, Billy, children do grow up fast and you can't stop it – but you can love them throughout. Oh, and bear in mind I love them even more than you do and I *will* watch over them every step of the way. When you say that a new child being on the way is, 'a bit rich!', I think I agree. It's a little bit of the richness of the tapestry of life that you will thank me for in years to come. How about trying a smile and rejoicing at the fact that life is indeed 'a wheelbarrow full of surprises', not dull and never meant to be. Have you ever looked at what it says in the good book that husbands should do for their wives? Give everything up if need be. Isn't that what Jesus did? Now, you've rightly identified that as a stretch. Though of course I would like to point out to you that it's the woman who gets the stretch marks! Loving unselfishly, like Jesus, is a huge stretch for all human beings. But Helen needs your love, your affirmation and your encouragement right now like never before.

You want Helen to shine? Well, in marriage, what you give her she shines right back at you. If she is tired, isn't it possible that she's showing you what you are showing her: 'I'm too tired for all this! I've already had three kids! I'm 50 and I can't be bothered! So I'm going into my cave and I'm going to sulk until the child is 20 and I might come out then!'? Honestly, my dear son, I don't think you really want to be like that. So how about turning this around? Instead of it being all about you, think about your beautiful, darling Helen, and show her a smiling face full of approval. Guess what will come back at you!

By the way, she's absolutely right about the children. They are, as you said, pretty smart. It's time to tell them!

As for a change of career, I have, as always, many ideas. When you were conceived I put things into you that have not yet been fulfilled or even dreamed of. So, here's my question: What's on your heart? What is it you'd really love to do? It's time to start dreaming. Let me know what you come up with.

Always your loving Dad,

GOD

PS Surely we're past sulking?

JUNE 21st

Dear God,

Well I read your letter – I winced at parts and laughed at others. Challenging as always. On that you *never* disappoint. But kind and firm and in an odd way strangely uplifting. Sometimes I wish you'd just let me wallow for a bit. After I'd had time to digest and, indeed, stomach the contents, I sat down with Helen and we talked it all out until the wee small hours over a bottle. She of course was not drinking but well ... you know me. I shared my fears and she in turn shared some of her concerns. One of which is my health. She wants me to cut back on the alcohol and take up some exercise. Worse still, she went to a local school fete and won three fitness sessions with a personal trainer. He's an African guy from Bradford. Seems OK but talks funny!

We told the children by the way, all pretty excited about it, with the exception of Tom who stomped up to his room, shouting about how he didn't have enough personal space as it was and how was he going to sleep with a baby crying all day and all night? I didn't point out that as he came home most mornings between 2 and 3 it would be only half the night anyway, but he has a point I suppose. (It won't be 24-7, will it? Will it?) Actually I'm worried about Tom. I don't partic- ularly like the gang he's hanging round with – they're not really bad kids, I don't think, just middle-class spoilt brats. He's been all over the place though recently; if he was a girl I'd put it down to PMT. But it's more than that. He is either quiet and melancholic or loud and abusive. The latter mostly

at the weekends when he comes home just as dawn is breaking having been out with his, 'mates'. I generally fall asleep in
front of the fire and wake when he comes in. I don't judge
him, though; I simply say 'I love you, son', whatever time it is.
And once he's made it safely to bed, I stagger upstairs and
join Helen.

I'm doing my best to honour her, you know, and try to
listen as much as possible and not make sarcastic remarks –
but the truth is I see the funny side of most things . . .

Anyway, must dash. I'm going for a job interview with
Hertfordshire constabulary. I know, PC Plod and all that . . .
but actually it's a little more complicated than that. All hush-
hush and on the down-low if you get my drift?

Love,

Billy

JUNE 23rd

Hello Billy,

Now, about the job in the police force: that's the old Billy trying to big himself up again, isn't it? Oh yes, it was 'plain clothes' I suppose. But a civilian assistant in the control room is more *Postman Pat* than *Miami Vice*, surely? When will you learn? It's a waste of time trying to impress me. It doesn't work. I know the truth and my dreams for you are real, not fantasy. On a more positive note, I'm glad you and Helen finally sat down and talked things through together. A glass of wine can help in these situations. It is why I gave the gift of wine – to gladden people's hearts. It's good that you shared your fears and even better that you were able to hear her concerns.

Helen has watched you over the last few weeks and become increasingly concerned at the way in which the bottle has become a refuge for you. If you continue down that path, you commit yourself to a terrible lie. Moses, my face-to-face friend, knew thousands of years ago that I was and am the only totally reliable support and the ultimate place of security. Replace me with a bottle and you'll discover nothing but torment.

Besides, Helen's right – you do need the exercise. In fact, you've needed it for years. You see, I have plans for you. I am in this with you for the long haul and I want you to commit yourself to that long haul with me. If you go to these fitness sessions, you might even find you enjoy them. The fitness trainer is an old friend of mine and I think he'll be a very good friend to you. You might like to remember that there is nothing wrong with a regional accent. My son and his friends came from Galilee so when they visited the cosmopolitan city of Jerusalem, their 'northern' accent meant they stood out like sore thumbs.

It was time you told the children. I'm glad they are excited. They should be. You know, even Tom will secretly be excited. But of course there is the teenage desire to be cool, and his fears of teasing from his mates forced him into the 'exit stage left' tantrum. There's no doubt about the power of friends at his age. The ringleader of the group, as you well know, is bitter and angry as well as very clever and manipulative. Tom has to see that for himself. Keep on praying for him. Your prayers and unconditional love will do more to keep him from the dangers of various chemical dependencies than anything else.

I'm glad you're seeking to honour Helen – just don't do it as a task. Take the time occasionally to sit and watch her, look at her and see how beautiful she really is, see how this baby is causing her to bloom. She won't always feel like that of course. As the months go by she will start to wonder whether you still see her as truly gorgeous. Let your love grow stronger as the bump grows larger!

Love,

Dad (GOD)

JUNE 25th

Hi God,

It's me – Tom. Sorry I haven't been in touch. Things are really tough and it's so unfair. Mum and Dad are all loved up and stuff. Having a baby. At their age. I mean it's disgusting. Wrinkly sex my mates call it. My mate Ron says it should be banned for the over-fifties and I think he's right! And surely they could be quieter. Sometimes Mum even shouts your name out really loud. Are you in there with them too? Because if you are – can you tell them to shut up, God, 'cos they're doing my head in! Oh and there's something else: I've got this mate who's started smoking weed and eating the odd 'magic mushroom'. Do you think there's anything wrong with that? I mean you created all this stuff and they're just herbs right? Like oregano and stuff. Let me know.

Tom

JUNE 27th

Hi there Tom,

It's very good to hear from you again. As you rightly say, it's been a while. I'm sorry you're finding this so tough. I'm going to ask you to make allowances for your mum and dad. Don't forget that for a long time they've each been locked inside a cage, trying to love each other while at the same time protecting themselves by remaining inside. Can you see how frustrated and lonely that would make them?

Now they have found the courage to come out of their cages and drop their pretence. They've discovered that what they have is beautiful. You may think they are wrinklies, but actually they are living the dream of young love, a dream that they never found when they were young. I find it rather touching. By the way, don't tell your mum you've characterised her as an 'over-fifty'. I think she would be quite annoyed. However, when it comes to the shouting, don't worry about Ron's opinion. Would you rather your parents were still as screwed up as they were? Would you want them to be as filled with bitterness and hatred towards each other as *Ron's* mum and dad are?

Why not have a quiet word with your mum and tell her, 'It's great that you and Dad are all loved up, and deep inside I'm really pleased about the baby (don't tell my mates!) but, Mum, do me a favour – shut the bedroom door. I honestly don't want to hear everything.' I think you'll find she'll be understanding. By the way, you asked me a question. Yes, of course I'm in there with them. Sex was my idea from the very beginning. When two people are engaged in making love inside the covenant love of marriage, it thrills my heart.

Thanks for asking me about the weed and the magic mushrooms. You're right, I did create them. Everything has its purpose, but it's not all for humans to eat or drink. Mercury is very valuable for human beings, but if you drink it, it would cause immense damage and might kill you. Strychnine has its uses even in medicine, but it must be strictly controlled because taken wrongly, it's lethal. Marijuana contains substances that can be of value, but smoking it is dangerous on a spiritual level, as are magic mushrooms – not to mention the threats to mental health.

I created human beings to know me by knowingly choosing relationship with me. The choice operates by a balance of mind, heart and spirit. You know you've got intellect and emotions. My Spirit speaking into your spirit gives a power of choice by which human beings become their most God-like. They can freely choose to enter into relationship with their Creator. I will only get into relationship with somebody on that basis. Marijuana and magic mushrooms bypass the filter of the intellect and hijack human emotions, opening them to any influence to invade their souls and take up residence there.

Tom, please remember I have an enemy who hates me. He knows just how much I love you. I am really your Dad, you know. I knew you before you were born, loved you from before the world existed. My enemy knows that. He will apply any pressure he can to get you to do those drugs

52

so he can march in, take up residence, fill you with the pollution of his lies and make it much more difficult for you to hear my voice. He will do all that because he knows that destroying you would give me immense pain. So the answer to your question, Tom, is quite simple – yes, I did make those things but not to be used in the way your 'mate' is using them. He will pay a heavy price. Fair enough? Stay in touch.

Always your loving Dad in deepest heaven,

GOD

PS Don't forget I'm wilder and more exciting than anything my enemy can come up with and anything your mates can dream of.

JUNE 29th

Dear Dad,

About applying to join the police, well, maybe it was just because I fancied doing something a little different. However, when I finally received a letter back, they told me they had given it to a stronger candidate. I'm guessing I was just too old! The ruddy cheek of it. I thought fifty was the new forty? So it's back to the drawing board for me. I suggested to Helen that I should perhaps become a 'man of the cloth', but she dissolved into peals of laughter for twenty minutes, at the end of which she said, 'I don't really see you in a dress with a funny hat on.'

I'm becoming increasingly worried about Tom: he's surly and uncommunicative – now I know this is not unusual for teenagers, but there's got to be something more to it. He's talking about getting a tattoo done, and Helen is beside herself with it all, which can't be doing her or our baby any good. Physically though she seems to be blooming . . . and for the most part she's sleeping OK. She does get a bit moody though sometimes. Annabel and Jack seem to be doing fine; Annabel has joined the local pony club and now goes out hacking with girls called Arabella and Camilla and keeps asking if we can buy her a horse. The only nag I ever invested in was called, 'Champion'. It was anything but, and I only owned a leg of it anyway. The damn thing never won and cost me over twenty grand in total. Jack is football mad and from time to time after lots of physio I do manage to kick a ball about with him. He's got what the talent scouts call 'a useful right foot'. More than can be said for me! Speaking of which I can hear him calling me from the garden. Will be in touch soon.

Love,

Billy

JUNE 30th

Dear Billy,

Why, oh why, are you still trying to pull the wool over my eyes? Of course you knew you wouldn't make it into the police in any capacity, not with your record. And it's not really your skill set is it? After all, you're not exactly Inspector Morse. Not even Sergeant Lewis!

When it comes to you thinking about becoming a minister in the church, Helen's laughter might have felt unkind but she does know you better than anybody else! You also might like to know that 'wearing a dress' is not necessarily vital these days. And you are, I think, unlikely to rise to a point where you would be required to wear a 'funny hat', unless of course you join a circus.

But here's something you do need to think about. Lots of men and women who follow Jesus overlook the fact that when they commit their work or everyday tasks to me, they become priests every bit as much as those who wear a bit of plastic round their necks – often more so! The main job of ministers in the church is to equip every member to become an agent of my Good News every day – in the family, in the workplace. Then, wherever they go, they will be little extensions of the kingdom of heaven. So, I would like you to take a step back. At this moment it's not about finding another job, it's more about committing yourself to hear the call that I've placed deep inside you. I have a dream for you and it's not so much about the job you do as about what I want you to become. The job will flow out of the calling. Discerning the calling is the tough thing. It requires honesty and a ruthless determination to discount everything that isn't true to what you are. You may think you're Fidget by name, Fidget by nature ... but I'm telling you, if you stay still in my presence long enough, you will become aware again of a dream that you once had and then wrote off, 'I could never do that. People like me don't do stuff like that. I'm just not good enough.'

When you reach that memory, you will find that I am there waiting to deny the lie. I will be ready to say, 'People like you *are* capable of things like that, and I'm the one who makes it possible.' I understand your concern for Tom. Don't try to 'fix' him. Whatever you try he will resist. Mind you, there will be moments when he may offer you a window of opportunity, a moment when he wants to know, 'Do you still love me, Dad, in spite of the fact I'm behaving like a real prat?' If you keep on praying and giving him to me in trust and love, when that moment comes you'll be able to say to him, 'Yes, son, I do still love you.'

Face it. He is a lot like you!

Treasure these days. Annabel is into horses now but soon she will be a beautiful young woman giving you worries of another kind. As for Jack, treasure this as well. You are at that moment in his life when he thinks you are truly amazing. Enjoy it! Who knows how long it will last?

As for you – take the time, find the place to be still and discover deep within you the impossible dream. I will be waiting right there.

Your ever-loving,

Dad

JULY 1st

Dear God,

You talk about 'the call' and 'the impossible dream' and discovering you in the stillness. It's hard, though – to discern where to go and what to do when we all seem to live our lives at 100 mph. But I am sure you are right about treasuring these moments.

Right now, I guess I need to focus on my family. My wife and children. To see this new child arrive and support Helen in the pregnancy – sustain my relationship with Tom, Annabel and Jack and try to get the balance right between being protective and allowing them the freedom to grow. Always a tricky one that. Do we have to let our children make mistakes? I know, you've seen me cock things up on a regular basis but it is painful to watch.

If only you didn't set such high standards! But Haakon shows it's possible. He's been like a good dad for me. Maybe there's hope for me as well – maybe. Like it says in your book, we have to keep pressing on to win the prize. But some things are tricky, like telling the truth. Helen is getting more and more voluminous by the day. She asked me the other day, 'Does my bum look big in this?' The truthful answer was, 'Yes it does, if it were any bigger you could get harpooned by a passing whaling fleet!' But it's important to be sensitive isn't it? So I said she looked 'lovely' but the dress she was wearing wasn't my favourite and didn't look as nice as the floaty maroon kaftan she sometimes wears with her mother's pearl necklace and earrings. I know it wasn't the perfect

58

answer but maybe what she wanted to hear. What do you think, Dad?

Love,

Billy

JULY 2nd

Billy, my son,

Yes, I talk about 'the call' to remind you that deep within you lies an impossible dream, because I believe in you. I want you to live the destiny I planned for you. It's right to focus on your family, your beautiful wife and children. But, the inheritance you pass on to them is more than just money and houses. It's a destiny fulfilled, a life rich with my presence and my approval. *That* is truly something for them to inherit. The only way they can do that is if you make time in the midst of all the rushing around to be still, listen to my voice and discover the call I've placed on you. If you don't do that, they'll grow up avoiding me just like you did. I want them to think you are more than just a good bloke. I want them to say, 'Once my dad was a plonker, but now, he's truly awesome.'

The best thing they can see is that you are a man with a vision that's even bigger than the family. They need to know they are your top priority. They also need to know you have your eyes fixed on an even greater prize. If they see that light in your eyes, it'll kindle the same thing in them – the longing to live a life of significance. If you, Fidget the fixer, the guy who lives his life at 100 miles an hour, think it's worth stopping and being still to hear the call of your heavenly Dad, then they'll get the idea, that the energy, adventure, excitement and thrill of living come from interaction with me.

When it comes to watching our children make mistakes,

I'm with you – it is painful. But there's an old promise full of ancient wisdom that says, 'Bring up a child in the way he should go and when he is old he will return to it.' That's worth remembering, especially when your children hit the teenage years and venture into the asteroid belt of cosmic stupidity. Then you will really need to walk close to me and trust my promise. Regarding Helen's dress and her question, your answer was pretty good. But next time she asks, take a moment to *really* look at her, see the years of faithful love and remember the light in her eyes when she tells you she loves you. Let her know that in your universe there is no more beautiful woman. That's not only what she *wants* to hear but *needs* to hear. Well done, my son. Stay close. You are going to need my strength.

Still and forever,

Your loving Dad

JULY 3rd

Dear God,

I'm exhausted and just feel like history is repeating itself. The police have just left – Billy is beside himself and is threatening to, 'Beat the living daylights out of you – you little shit!!

It seems that Tom wasn't just hanging out with the wrong peer group at school so much as being the ringleader. Now he's been caught dealing marijuana. The school quite rightly have a zero tolerance policy towards anything like that and so he has been expelled. Slap bang in the middle of his A levels. Bang go his dreams of studying law at uni! And as he was dealing, he will be charged – a date has been set for the initial hearing – just two weeks before our baby's due . . . Annabel was very upset when the police came charging in and Jack fled to his room shouting, 'Don't let them take Tom away! He's my brother!' I'm going to waddle upstairs in a minute to try and stop Billy from throttling Tom.

Dear God, what is going to become of us?

Love,

Helen xx

JULY 3rd

MIDNIGHT

Phone call

Haakon: Hello?

Billy: Haakon, I'm so glad you're there.

Haakon: Ah, Billy. How are things?

Billy: Not good. Our son's just been arrested for dealing dope. Not just a little bit either. I haven't managed to get the whole story yet. But he's in lots of trouble. Even though it's really early days, I think he's probably going to go to prison. He's right in the middle of his A levels. All his dreams of becoming a lawyer go out the window. Worst of all, I lost my rag totally. I really thought at one point that I was in danger of killing him. I was so angry. He's my son and I was so angry – and scared. There's no one else I can trust like you. So I hope you don't mind me calling you?

Haakon: Of course I don't mind. Why do you think you were so angry?

Billy: Because he's like me. It's the sort of stunt I would have pulled at his age if we'd had drugs around in the same way. He's like me, and that scares me. What am I going to do, Haakon?

Haakon: Billy, you're going to do what you always do. Eventually you're going to talk to your heavenly Father. And you're going to give him your boy. You're going to hand him over and say, 'This is too big for me, Dad. I'm giving you my boy. Watch over him please. Do what you say you do. Turn this around and make it for good even though I can't see how it can be.' That's what you're going to do, because you are a man of God.

Billy: I don't feel much like a man of God at the moment. No man of God has become as utterly furious as I was. Haakon, I was totally out of control.

Haakon: Ah, but you weren't. You didn't kill him. You felt like it, but you didn't. That's encouraging isn't it?

Billy (chuckling): I suppose it is. But it's scary, Haakon. It really is. How will it end up? What's going to happen?

Haakon: I don't have that kind of insight, Billy. All I know is our heavenly Father is better at working these things out so that they become a blessing, not a curse, than anyone else I know. So we have to trust him, don't we?

Billy: Yes, we do. Thank you so much for saying 'we'.

Haakon: Why wouldn't I? I'm your dad aren't I? That's what we agreed.

Billy: Yes, you are, aren't you? I have to say I'm really bloody glad about that. Forgive the language.

Haakon: That's OK. I understand. Trust the Father, Billy. Trust the Father. He is big enough to cope.

Billy: Thanks. Thank you so much. I'm going to try. Keep praying for me won't you?

Haakon: You know I will – always.

Billy: Bye then, and thanks.

JULY 4th

Helen, dearest daughter,

I know it's difficult, and you are exhausted. Stop. Remind yourself that I truly am your Father and my love is wrapped all around you. Take a moment to stay in the place of being loved. Our enemy wants to rob you of that. Don't let him do it. Of course, you know why Billy is so angry, don't you? It's because he feels horribly guilty. He thinks this is part of the toxic inheritance he has passed on to his son. He is only partially right. Every human being has inherited – through the long family line of the human race – the tendency to rebellion, selfishness and stupidity. Tom is no exception! Just don't give up on him. He needs to know two things: firstly, that you love him unconditionally; secondly, that you are deeply disappointed and ashamed of his actions *but* still proud of him as a son. That's my heart and you're going to need to draw on it.

You're right about the consequences of being discovered. Certainly in the short term it's going to mess up all his great plans and wreck his dreams. But the action that's been taken gives him a chance to recognise how stupid he's been plus an opportunity to discover what my destiny is for him. Keep on praying for him. Don't forget repentance is the key to discovering my kingdom purpose. And I definitely have a destiny for Tom, a dream that is bang in the centre of my heavenly kingdom's purpose on earth. I know this is a huge test *and* coming at a moment when you are already facing a rather big challenge! Just love

Annabel and Jack. Don't hide from them the fact that Tom's been monumentally stupid. But don't hide from them either the fact that you still love him and they should too. As to what shall become of you, some bad things will happen, but trust me: my love and my grace are bigger than all the plans of our enemy and even bigger than the stupidity of your son. I will pull you all through this. Just trust me. Make time in the middle of it all to remember you are my daughter, loved, honoured and gloriously beautiful. Take those moments to let me love you. That will strengthen you more than anything else you can experience.

Always your loving Dad,

GOD

JULY 5th

Hello God – it's me.

I guess you've seen what's happened. I wasn't entirely truthful. It wasn't just my mate who was involved with drugs. I've been nicked for 'Possession and intent to supply' marijuana. I've got to go to court. Thing is, I can't bring myself to tell Mum and Dad just how I got all the stuff. But you know – in fact you knew all along in spite of what you put in your last letter. You could have warned me.

I thought Dad was going to kill me. He was so incredibly angry. It's all Ron's fault really: we met this mate of his called Wilf in our local pub; he worked at the garden centre. Turns out he'd been doing more than his fair share of moonlighting and needed somewhere to store his crop of harvested marijuana. Ron said he knew of this derelict house and asked me to help him stash the stuff there. Said I could help myself any time. Problem was, Wilf had been stealing fertiliser and one day was caught red-handed by the manager. Me and Ron tried to sell as many bags of grass as we could to get them out of the way. But then our sixth form head caught me red-handed dealing to some Year 11 girls. That's when the police were called in. I'm frightened, God. Will they really 'Lock me up and throw away the key' like Dad says?

Help me. PLEASE.

Love,

Tom

JULY 6th

Dear Tom,

Yes, I know what's happened and no, you haven't been entirely truthful. That's a very economical way of describing things. You lied to me by leaving out large parts of the truth. 'I've got a friend who is doing this' is one of the oldest tricks in the book. Of course I knew. But I'll tell you what I've said to your dad many times. I can't work with lies, only with the truth. I can't work with what I know about you, only what you tell me. You've got to be straight with me. If you read the last letter I sent, I *did* warn you. I told you your 'mate' will pay a heavy price. Turns out that's you. Now it's time to pay the piper.

Remember, I warned you that my enemy, who's also your enemy, has only one aim in mind. He wants to destroy you. I want to protect you but I can only do that if you'll trust me. Do you remember what I wrote: 'I'll only have a relationship with somebody when they consciously and freely open themselves up to me'? It's your call. You tell me your dad was incredibly angry. Of course he was. He loves you. You know he does. Have you forgotten the way he put his life on the line to rescue you from Eddie Fast? Seeing you embark on a path of self-destruction is ripping him apart.

And it's even more complicated. He feels, because of his own lifestyle in the past, that this must be his fault. But you and I know this was your choice. Even when you're talking about it, there's a note of self-congratulation and

'Aren't I a lad?' Part of you still wants to claim it's a bit of a laugh. But what you don't know is that one of the people you sold that stuff to will pay the real price: he is on the brink of developing schizophrenia. So you think you've played the Big Man – but you are right to be frightened. I won't tell you what they'll do when you come up before the court. You've asked me to help you, and I will – because I love you. Your gifts of leadership, creativity, imagination and your sense of adventure have all been put to wrong use in this incident. I gave you those gifts because I love you. I have such big dreams for your life. I don't want you to miss them – that would be truly stupid. Which way are you going to go?

Let me know.

Your loving heavenly Dad,

GOD

JULY 15th

Dear God,

Well, talk about chickens coming home to roost! I know Helen's been in touch and told you what Tom has gone and done. The apple never falls too far from the tree does it? And I just feel so massively guilty – I was a lousy role model for him as a dad and now he's gone and got himself busted for dealing weed.

The date's set now for the trial at the Crown Court so we've had to get him a brief and get on with it.

We were recommended a bloke by the name of Donald Harbinger, seems like a nice chap and well-connected too – his dad sits in the High Court. So it's likely we'll use him. He told Tom straight up that even with a first-time offence, given that he was 'in possession with intent to supply' it is likely that, barring a miracle, he will go to a young offenders' institution, and then on to one of Her Majesty's prisons when he turns eighteen in a few months. So . . . he's looking at anything from two to five years and that's with a guilty plea . . . plus it has been recommended that Tom goes to a drugs counselling service.

I haven't been this scared since I was in the lock-up with Eddie Fast. If he gets sent down our access to him will be very limited and I'm deeply concerned he'll come out of this a full-scale villain. The other thing is, I'm worried about the effect this is having on Helen and our unborn child. She's been getting worse than usual stomach cramps and we're going in for another scan next week – she says it doesn't feel right inside . . .

I've called out to you before. We both know it – and you have always come through. Now I need you to – more than ever before.

So, help me God. Please.

Love,

Billy

JULY 16th

My dear son Billy,

Of course I know what Tom's done. Helen shared with me the anger you feel. There's nothing wrong with that. You're angry because he's your boy and you love him dearly. How could you not be enraged? It's blatantly self-destructive behaviour. But not all your anger is wholesome. Some of it is rage and despair springing from your own history. You say you feel massively guilty. That will not help. It will poison your dealings with him. Think about it. Yes, you were a lousy role model for him, once. But as you allowed me to walk with you and begin to change you, you learned to be forgiven. You began to see yourself through my eyes. It changed everything. It cut the thread of poisonous self-loathing. You started to love, especially to love yourself. You became totally different. Hold on to that lesson now.

Remember what I said to you before – Tom is a lot like you. I remember the young Billy who used to try and look up the skirts of the choir mistress. I loved you then and have never stopped. Even through your years of bitterness and rage, when you selfishly used everyone you came across, I never gave up on you. You know why. I am your real Dad. Now it's time to reflect that towards Tom. Are you going to be like me? Are you going to go on loving him? Is he going to see a smile on your face that reaches your eyes and comes from deep inside? Is he going to get from you the sense that you believe in him and will never give up on him? After all, that's the way I've treated you.

Believe it or not, it is possible for him to see my face in your face.

Well done for taking the right steps and getting Tom a good brief. Whenever you think about him, remember how I have followed you and loved you down the years. Know this – I am doing exactly the same with him. Keep on entrusting him to me. No matter what happens, I am the God who rescued you. I'm still the same, and I will rescue Tom. I know that might feel impossible with him on remand right now. But he will come to the point where he learns, like you did, that no matter how much he twists and turns and ducks and dives, he has to face reality. And he has to make a choice about the ultimate reality – me. You're right about prisons, often they are 'Universities of Crime'. But don't forget I'll be there and even if you find it hard to believe, some of the lads in there are my boys. I won't stop watching over Tom.

In the middle of all this, I'm glad you're not forgetting Helen. A crisis like this in the family will often have an impact on the physical well-being of its members. It's the way I've made you as human beings. In this case, Helen has internalised all this. But I'm watching over her too.

Remember what I've said in desperate situations before – trust me with this. Keep on seeing me as standing above it all, and I do. I am the God of all things, Maker of the whole Universe. Every single atom is mine. Helen knows what I've promised; I'm always working for your good in everything I do.

Your loving Dad,

GOD

73

SEPTEMBER 7th

Helen, my dearest daughter,

I have often said it before. I love your letters because they are so honest. I know you've been trying to find peace. Well done. But you're trying too hard. You can't get it that way. It's a gift to be received. From me. Just stop, and accept it. I know that's hard. It's almost impossible to stop running frantically on the inside, when you're rushing about trying to deal with the home and coping with the situation you've been thrown into by Tom's foolishness. But you have to do it.

So: take precious moments of time to stop. Breathe. Know that I am God. Not just a nice idea, but the truth. Be still – allow my presence to wrap itself around you. When you've let that happen, give me your fears and worries about the baby. Remember, I know Tom and the baby and love them even more than you do. What's coming will be painful. As I told you ages ago, walking with me is not always easy. But it is companionable. I walk with you every day. Think about what you wrote – the pain of living with Billy and all his sordid past *was* turned around. Joy did come as you moved into relationship with me and your extended family was restored to you. Believe it and trust. This baby *is* going to be a massive delight to you. Trust in me. Don't allow the despair to take over. Be careful how you think and how you express your thoughts. You wrote 'and now finally this'. Dear daughter, this is not 'finally'. It is a passing trouble. It will be painful but it's not the final word on your life or on the family. Even if Tom goes to jail it will not be a *finally* for you, for him or the family. I am bigger than that. Trust me, if he goes to jail, I will be there. I have my servants in there. Where am I? I am in the middle of it all – with you. I promised you I will never leave you, never forsake you. That is my promise forever. I know it's hard, but please do what I asked – be still long enough for my presence to pour peace into you. I am there even if you cannot feel me.

Your loving Father in deepest heaven,

GOD

SEPTEMBER 9th

God – it's me Tom.

I'm terrified. Mum's not well. Dad is blaming me. He's told me Annabel and Jack won't stop crying. And I'm up before the Crown Court in a couple of days. I'm frightened what will happen to me if I go 'inside'. I'm pleading guilty and my brief seems to have done the best he can, but I'm afraid that I will end up with a 'custodial sentence', that's what he calls it I think. And yes, I'm sorry. Very sorry. Sorry for the pain I've caused Mum and Dad and also for the fact that I heard yesterday that one of the lads, you know, Kevin? He came to Mum and Dad's thing . . . Well, he bought weed off me and apparently he decided he could fly and leapt off the top of the Sixth Form centre. He crushed the lower part of his legs and it is likely he'll be in a wheelchair for the rest of his life. What an almighty mess. How can I ever live with myself?

Love,

Tom

PS I am doing my best to be brave for everyone but all I really want is for Mum and Dad to hold me like a little baby and tell me it's all going to be all right. I'm missing them tonight like I've never missed them before.

SEPTEMBER 10th

Hello Tom,

It's good to hear from you – especially to have a letter from you that's honest about how you really feel. I know you're terrified. Just don't allow that to control you. It's natural to worry about your mum but remember how much I love her. Instead of just worrying, why not pray? You used to know how to. Give her to me and give the baby to me, because I love them and believe it or not, I love you.

I know your dad is blaming you, but don't forget what I told you before: he's actually blaming himself as well. What you've done will have real consequences. When you go to Crown Court, don't just think about yourself. Think about your mum. And about your dad. He's still the same man who ran into the garage to face Eddie Fast and his men all just to get back his son. So give them to me and give thanks for them because you are truly lucky to have such parents.

It's true your dad was a rogue in the past. But he had the guts to turn his life around. Faith does take guts. He turned to me, listened to me and you know what happened as a result. So when you're at the Crown Court, remember this – I am there with you. Whatever happens, in all that happens, I am working for your good because I love you.

You are scared of what might happen to you in prison. Here's where you have to grow up fast. You have to walk with me, listen to my voice and trust me – that means doing what I say, without hesitation! I'll be there. I will never leave you alone. Well done for recognising that you've caused your mum and dad lots of pain. When it comes to your pal Kevin, his legs are badly damaged, but you know he could have died. He is alive and he has hope. He is someone else you need to be praying for. Give him to me. Don't try and carry the burden of that guilt on your own. It will just crush you. Keep on every day giving Kevin to me. You're making a good beginning. You're starting to care for others and often that's the first step on the road that leads to what you really need – redemption.

I love you, Tom. I am genuinely proud that you're trying to be brave. Don't forget this if you are sent down, your mum and dad will come and say goodbye to you and they will have to leave. They will hug you and go. They will feel completely heartbroken. You'll feel utterly bereft and alone. But you won't be alone. I will be with you. I will make myself real to you if you reach out to me. One last thing to say, you called it an almighty mess. There is only one thing in the Universe that is almighty and that's me. This thing is huge and nasty. But I am bigger. If you want me to be, I am your loving and eternal Dad in deepest heaven and right next to you. Don't let go of that.

Father GOD

SEPTEMBER 12th

Dear God,

I think today has been the worst day of my life. Tom pleaded guilty in front of the beak. Our barrister, Mr Harbinger, did a great job citing our family circumstances, and the fact that Tom had never been in trouble before. He even called our vicar Colin as a character witness, but it made no difference. They sent my boy down. For three years. He's off to the young offenders' institution. The judge said in the circumstances he was being lenient. Well, it didn't feel like it. Tom did his best to be brave. He didn't say anything when he was sentenced. Just stared at us from the dock with rivers of tears flooding down his cheeks. His mother managed to squeeze his hand before he was taken down, and then he was gone. We got in the car and Helen screamed hysterically and clutched her tummy. Our child is not ready to be born yet! Why is this happening? I drove straight to the hospital, and so right now I'm sitting outside the hospital room waiting to find out what's happened. They said normally I'd be allowed in but because it's an emergency I'm stuck here. Oh God, help me! Help us! My poor wife. My son! What is going to happen to us?

Billy

SEPTEMBER 13th

Billy, my son,

If I say to you that I know exactly how you feel, will you believe me? When my Son was on trial, not even the fact that he was completely innocent made a difference and he wasn't just sent down but sentenced to death. Believe me, I understand the tears of pain and the agony of having to watch. Can I gently challenge you on something? This day has not been the worst day of your life. It may be the most painful and most heart-breaking. But you have acted honourably and with compassion towards your son. As I see it, the worst day of your life was the day you raped Sara. Today was one of the best days. I was more proud of you today than I've ever been before. One day I will show you it from my perspective and you will see why I say this is one of the best days of your life.

Even Tom rose above himself. He thought of you and Helen and did his best to act in a way that would reassure you and also make you proud. It may not seem like it, but he has begun the journey that will take him from where he has been into the fine young man I made him to be. I promise you now, one day your boy will make you so proud, it will leave you breathless.

For Helen, the situation has been devastating. When she knew her boy was going away for three years, it was like a sword through her. The pain is the price we pay for loving. Remember my Son, crying out from the cross, 'My God, My God, why have you abandoned me?' Those words left a wound in me and in him, a wound that has bound us together even more than before. That wound has enabled us to offer healing to wounded relationships ever since. Nothing is wasted.

Your pain as you think about Helen and contemplate what may be happening to her is part of the price you are paying for the real relationship, the genuine heartfelt love you share with her. Surrender her to me, trust me, I will work this out for the best. And your boy is in my hands.

'What is going to happen to us?' you ask. You will come out of these terrible events more 'us' than ever before, more truly family, bound in love to each other more than you could ever have been if this had not happened. It's what I do, you see: I take the vile attacks of my enemy on those who love me, and turn those attacks around. Out of them I bring joy and glory.

Here's what I want you to do – hang on, hang on to me, cling to me literally for dear life. I will not let you down.

Your loving Father in deepest heaven,

GOD

SEPTEMBER 13th

Oh God.

  It's totally degrading. I was taken down, handcuffed, shoved into a tiny cubicle in this van with a slit for a window and driven off at speed with the other 'young lags' to the prison. They took all my clothes off me, made me bend over (which was really scary) parted the cheeks of my bum and then shone a torch up there in case I was 'carrying anything'. All the while they were making lewd jokes about what was going to happen to me 'inside'. Then they made me don a boiler suit, took all my possessions away and man-handled me into a cell where they threw open the door and said, 'Here, Lefty. Got a new recruit for you.' Do you know why he's called that? Because his left eye is so stigmatised it turns in toward his nose. The first thing he said was, 'What you looking at?' He must weigh about 20 stone, is as ugly as sin and turns eighteen in three weeks' time. And the cell. Apart from the fact it stinks of poo and piss, the walls are covered from floor to ceiling in porn. It is impossible not to see it. I am literally shitting myself with fear, which is terrible as we don't get to 'slop out' until the morning and Lefty is well pissed off. He keeps shouting for the guards and saying if they don't come he's going to 'do' me.

  Help me, God. I am so frightened. I think I'm going to die in here.

  Love,

  Tom

SEPTEMBER 15th

Tom, my dear son,

I know it's degrading. That is why they do it to you, to break you down. The point is to rob you of your dignity and any sense of value in yourself. The jokes about what's going to happen to you, and the whole process, are designed to make you afraid. Why? Because they can. And for a few of them, guards and inmates alike, it's all they've got left in their lives – the ability to make others afraid. It's what they live for now.

Remember how exciting it felt to be breaking the rules your mum and dad set down for you? Selling weed to your mates. You were blurring the boundaries and creating a world in which you thought you could do what the hell you liked. When humans open the door to a world like that, what you wind up with is an experience like Lefty's going through now. Of course, not all offenders and prison guards are like that, but there are enough of the ones that are to create a culture of fear.

What do you want to do? You have a stark choice. Do you want to be part of that? Or do you want to walk my way? Lefty didn't start off hard, aggressive and ugly as sin. But he has grown a covering of hatred and aggression. Inside that armour plating is a fearful little lad who was bullied because his eye looked funny, until he learnt that he didn't have to take it. He could make them afraid. He grew to like it. Now it's who he is.

I said you would have to grow up fast. A wise man wrote long ago, 'Well-formed love banishes fear.' Love isn't a fuzzy feeling; it is a commitment to seek the best for the other guy, no matter what it may cost. I know you know that my Son faced something like that. You are in a place governed by fear. The only thing that's going to get you through is perfect love. I know that sounds like hearts and flowers and a load of garbage. But if you do what I'm asking, you can grasp hold of the only power that could change the culture of that place, and then you will get through. People in there know all about what they call bullshit (yes, I've heard of the word!). Because they know about that, they also know about the opposite – truth.

What do you think? Can you do it? Can you open yourself up to me and let my truth live in you, in the middle of the situation there? I told you, you are going to have to grow up fast. You don't have long to make the choice. I know there's part of you saying, 'How can that work? What do I do? What's going to happen if Lefty tries to "do" me?'

I will not desert you. Reach out. Listen to my voice and you *will* know. Open up, receive my life and my love. Do it now. Then do exactly what Lefty asks you to do. He said 'What you looking at?' Ask yourself what it would be like to have his life? Ask Jesus what his response would be. What would he see, looking at Lefty? Let him show you. Tell Lefty what you've seen. See what happens.

By the way, I've got plans for you and they do not involve you dying in there. So what have you got to lose?

Dear God,

I was reading your letter under the bedclothes last night. Lefty asked me what I was doing, so I told him. His first response was, 'You're off your rocker! Guards, I'm living with a nutter in 'ere. Get me out!' Then he started to laugh. He must have laughed for about fifteen minutes non-stop. Like a maniac. Finally, when he had subsided I said to him, 'Look, Lefty, right now all you and I have is this room, our bucket of slops and each other. The way I see it is we can choose to live the rest of our lives like this or we can do something about it.' I'll be honest, and God I know that might be a funny choice of word in my current circumstances, but as I spoke to Lefty the fear that I had been feeling about my incarceration and my relationship with him left me. I got a sort of . . . confidence. He said, 'What d'ya mean?' And I told him that I was going to start trusting in you and praying for a way out of this situation and then I said to him, 'Look, Lefty, are you in or out?' He laughed again but this time it was warmer and he said, 'I am in. In 'ere and yes I want out – so if this God pal of yours wants to help, I'm all for it.' Then he turned over, farted loudly and went to sleep.

Help me, God. I know I've done wrong. Hurt my parents. Put them under terrible pressure. And I think I've hurt you too. I am sorry. I know I deserve to be here and must pay the price, but please, please do not leave me alone. I'm going to try and trust you. Trust that together you, me and Lefty will find a way through this mess. I'm pretty sure you heard that 'cos I'm feeling all warm and fuzzy. I think I'll be all right tonight.

Thanks, God.

Love,

Tom

Good lad! Reading under the bedclothes was exactly what would intrigue Lefty. He's used to kids coming in with a letter from their mum, a note from their girlfriend or a few pages from a porn magazine. He would have ripped you to shreds if it had been any of those. He would have made you a laughing stock. But you told him straight who the letter was from. It caught him off guard and it spoke to something deep inside him. When he was a little kid and scared, he used to call out to me. I've tried to get messengers alongside him before. But you're the first who's managed it. You say you got a kind of confidence as you spoke to Lefty. It's a confidence that grows when you follow my guidance and speak my words. In fact, it's called something: faith.

I'll tell you something else. Not only did I hear, but the angels heard when you told him you were going to start trusting me and start praying. They were cheering, and cheering even louder when he gave you his reply and told you he wanted to be 'in' on all this. He's definitely going to discover that your pal God *wants* to help. Prayers like the one you prayed, turning back to me – raw, honest and costly – always result in angels dancing and joy erupting all over heaven. I'm glad you can see how much you've hurt your parents and now know how wrong that was. Yes, you've hurt me. But that's only possible because I truly love you just as your parents do, except that my love is bigger, stronger and, unlike theirs, eternal.

You're going to discover just how tough my love is. It's

like a cable made of twisted high-tensile steel. So, you already have my answer – I will never leave you alone! When you said 'I'm going to trust you,' you opened up a line of communication from heaven to earth and earth to heaven, and my love flowed in. That caused the wonderful sensation you felt. Your sleep that night was the gift of my Son, who has promised 'peace like the world can never give' to those who follow him. Now the adventure begins. Some of it will be tougher than anything you've ever faced. Some of it will be more amazing than anything you've ever experienced. But all the way through, here is my promise – I will never leave you.

Your Father in heaven,

GOD

SEPTEMBER 24th

Dear God,

I'm at the hospital again. They managed to keep Helen going for a couple of weeks so as to give Tiny a bit more of a chance, but today they decided they had to go in and get the baby out. The surgeon has just come out of theatre along with the paediatrician. They told me that during the Caesarian Helen had an allergic reaction to the anaesthetic and she is now in a critical state. The baby (a little girl) is tiny and having trouble breathing so she has been taken to their special care baby unit. I can't stand this, God. Am I going to lose her? What am I going to tell the children?

Billy

SEPTEMBER 25th

Billy, dear son,

First things first – don't tie yourself up in words like 'I can't stand this, God.' A declaration like that sits on you, wraps itself round you. It becomes a curse that binds up your whole being. The truth is, with me, you can and you will stand it, because I have put my nature in you and you will not fail. Yes, you may falter and you may even fall, but you will not fail, not with me.

That is what I want you to tell the children: 'Your mum has had an allergic reaction to the drugs and she is in great danger. But God is bigger and, kids, we're going to trust him. No matter what the doctors say, this is not her time to die. Your little sister has a special destiny in God. I don't believe God brought her into this world just so she could die. So, we're going to believe your mum will pull through and so will the baby. We're not in this alone. We're with God and when we walk with him, we always walk with the possibility of miracles.' As you speak out those words to them, words that have my truth in them, you will find that your heart is changed.

Don't forget, your Helen is someone over whom I've watched since she was born. I saw her struggling through childhood abuse and years of spiritual and emotional chains. I have not finished with her. She has yet to become the fully formed glorious jewel that she will be. That little girl has a special purpose on her. The enemy of all that is good would love to destroy her. But when your prayers are filled with faith, they join with my power and authority to form a shield he cannot penetrate. I'm inviting you to stand with me. Proclaim life over Helen and the little girl and together we will see the enemy run with his tail between his legs. Stand with me and this is a battle you will win. I didn't bring you this far to see you fail! Still believing in you.

Your loving Dad in deepest and highest heaven,

GOD

SEPTEMBER 26th

Dear God,

I did as you suggested, and last night sat down with Annabel and Jack and told them that we had to pray for Mummy, that yes she was seriously ill, but she wasn't going to die. We were all pretty tearful, especially little Jack who is genuinely bewildered by the absence of Tom. He keeps saying, 'But Tom's not *really* bad, Daddy!' And I say, 'I know Jack, but he has made a very serious mistake and has to spend some time away from us in prison where he's being made to think about what he did.' Do you know what he said when I told him that, 'But Daddy, that's just not fair ...' Where do you begin to explain the unfairness of this world to an eight-year-old boy?

Anyway, today when we went to the hospital, the three of us held hands in a circle beside Helen's bed as she lay there unconscious, and we proclaimed how much you love her, how much we love and need her and we started singing – and this is going to sound a little strange but we started singing, 'What a Wonderful World' – you know, the old Louis Armstrong classic? It was her mother's favourite record. Anyway, at the end of the song, as we sing the last line, 'And I say to myself what a wonderful world' she opens her eyes and she looks at me and whispers, 'Oh yeah'.

Next thing, the staff nurse rushes in and sees us all round the bed smiling and Helen mouthing 'I'd love a glass of water.' The nurse is wonderfully Irish and typically Catholic, and is amazed to see Helen conscious and trying to talk and

I hear her mutter under her breath, 'Jesus, a real life miracle' and I see water rise in her eyes and with it the restoration of a hope that years of nursing the chronically ill had maybe drained from her. She recovers quickly though and her training kicks in: 'Right ... wonderful ... can you all just step away from the bed please – the doctor will be here presently.'

So the doctor comes and then the consultant neurologist, and she's given another brain scan and more blood tests and they can find absolutely nothing wrong ... They're almost embarrassed by the whole thing and then finally the neurologist says, 'There is no logical explanation for what has happened here today. I am not a man of faith but I must simply assume that somebody, some power even, somewhere ... has a lot left for you to do. I am delighted for you Mrs Fidget and indeed for your whole family.' God – what a day. What a God! By the way, have I told you we've decided to call our little girl Liberty? Helen says it is because while she was, as she puts it, 'asleep' she saw your face and has never felt so free.

I love you.

Billy xxx

SEPTEMBER 27th

Billy,

Well done, son! You did what I asked. You spoke out words of faith and shared them with the children. As you did it, faith rose in you and you built in them a foundation of confidence in me. Like cynicism and disbelief, faith is contagious. I know Jack's tears and bewilderment come close to breaking your heart. The truth is, from his perspective, of course it is not fair. That's the problem with the whole issue of sin. Whenever anybody breaks the rules and steps outside the boundaries, someone else gets wounded. In this case, it's an eight-year-old boy called Jack. And his mother. But at least he has you to explain that although Tom may not be, in his eyes, really bad, what Tom did was truly wicked.

Help him understand that Tom's actions have resulted in lifelong damage and severe injury, and could have led to much worse. I think he will get it. Don't be afraid of explaining this to him. Don't forget, he hears my voice as well. I have to say how much I enjoyed your time of proclamation and faith at the hospital. Of course, I had a smile on my face because I knew what was going to happen. What you had done created one of the most powerful forces in the world. The pure and genuine faith of children is powerful. As you sang, faith arose in Helen so that she could say, 'Oh yeah!' The whole choir of angels repeated it by the way. You may remember when my Son was walking the earth, he had a reputation for spoiling funerals by raising the dead. Of course I heard what the nurse said and you were right, what happened in Helen's room has produced in her a resurrection of hope.

By the way, don't be surprised if the hospital manages to find a completely logical and natural 'explanation' for what's happened. In your culture, miracles always seem to produce embarrassment among professionals. Suffice it to say that the neurologist actually spoke my truth to you for Helen. There is a lot left for Helen to do. I love the idea of calling your daughter Liberty. By the way, did you ask the nurse what her name is? You might be interested. That time in a coma was vital for Helen. All her defences melted away and she saw my smile, truly saw it for the first time ever. Here's something you need to make sure of – tell Tom what has happened to his mum. He has been praying for her and it will lift from him a terrible burden.

Thank you for expressing your love. There is no greater gift that anyone can bring me. Just lie back in the warmth of my love, relax and rejoice. You have done brilliantly well.

Your loving Dad,

GOD

SEPTEMBER 28th

My dear son,

We have had some wonderful news. Your mum has regained consciousness and is now back to her usual bossy self! She's due to come out of hospital at the end of the week. We're all so excited that God answered our prayers.

Oh yes – and I have a message for you. She says, and I quote, 'Be sure to tell Tom I love him, and miss him and that none of this is his fault. Tell him just as soon as I'm able I'll be down to the young offenders' institution to visit him – and also tell him to stay strong and keep the faith – tell him, and this is important, Billy, tell him I still believe in him.' So there you go, Tom. We do still love you and *we* believe in you. This is not forever although it may feel that way. Your time will come. And when it does it will be *so* good.

We love you.

Dad

OCTOBER 1st

Dear God,

I'm excited about what you wrote in your last letter about Helen . . . that there's a lot for her still to do . . . there certainly is at the moment. Now Helen's home at last and Liberty is keeping us *very* busy. If she's not filling her nappies she's bawling at the top of her lungs. I'd forgotten just how intensive the first few weeks are!

She is a delight though, and has a wonderful gummy smile that reminds me of her mum, that and the tuft of gorgeous deep brown hair on her head. Jack and Annabel are very sweet with her, but there is something missing, an absence. Actually it is a dark chasm that is horribly painful, and I think it stems from the fact that Tom isn't here to share in our happiness. I've written to him and told him the good news and everything, and included a few words from his mum which I think could be significant . . . but as much as we're happy here, our eldest child is locked away, we can't talk to him except once a week for a few precious minutes on the phone, and neither can we hold him. And as his dad I feel utterly powerless to protect him. So the minutes, hours, days and nights are tinged with sadness . . . and at times it feels like he will never return to us.

But you lost a son didn't you? And so you and he are fully acquainted with the business of isolation. In a few days' time we're going to try and see Tom in prison – it should be an interesting visit. In his last letter home he said he'd experienced the Holy Spirit and not only that, but his cell mate Lefty appears to have had a change of heart about the life he's been leading and he has softened in his approach to our lad. I'll let you know how we all get on. Anyway, God, got to go now. I can hear Liberty crying and Helen's asleep so I'd better get some formula on the go. See you soon?

Love,

Billy x

PS I found out the nurse's name is Edith. You know, as in Edith Cavell? The heroine from the Great War that my grand-dad used to tell me about. So now our little girl is called Liberty Edith Fidget. Sweet, isn't it?

OCTOBER 3rd

Hello Billy,

Great to hear from you. I thought I'd answer your last question first! You ask, 'See you soon?' I think if you keep your eyes open and attuned to the signs of my presence, then, yes indeed, you will be seeing me soon. I'm delighted to know you feel excited about all I have in store for Helen.

Can I ask you to take a moment to reflect on something? It's not very long since you were writing, 'I can't stand this, God!' Now you are writing to tell me about your excitement. There's nothing wrong with that. What's happened to Helen is something to be excited about. But I want you to understand something very important – in all that was happening, I never changed. I am always the same. I have always loved you, always believed in you – and always will. It's something to bear in mind for the future. Circumstances may change, but my love, my utter commitment to you never changes. I am your Dad now and forever.

I am glad you are so happy with your little daughter. Rely upon it. She is not only keeping you very busy right now, but she's going to do that for many years. When you look down at her face and are overwhelmed with love for her, remember, that's how I look at you. By the way, I suggest you don't tell Helen that 'Liberty's gummy smile reminds me of her mum.' She might not get it!

I understand completely what you're talking about with Tom's absence. If you can imagine that feeling multiplied a million times, you would *begin* to know how I feel about the loss of any single person who refuses to come to me. Every one of them leaves a gap in my heart. But here's the thing: though Tom is away from the family in physical terms, he is actually closer to you now than he has ever been. Your letter to him was beautifully done. The message from his mum is of enormous power. It's going to be a huge encouragement to that young man. After all he has done, he needs to know, not only that you love him, but you still believe in him. It's so good that you allowed my Holy Spirit to speak through you when you said to him, 'Your time will come and when it does it will be so good.' You were speaking not only from your heart, but from mine too.

Isolation, now that's an interesting word. My Son and I at the time of the cross endured almost unbearable separation, but never isolation. You see, deep inside we were always united in purpose, even though we were separated by the task he had undertaken. Think about it, Tom is still in your heart isn't he? And aren't you now in his, now more than ever before all this happened? So don't forget, you're not alone; I am walking through this with you closer than I've ever been. The same applies to Tom. Don't be surprised if when you finally see him, there's a change.

Always your loving,

Dad

OCTOBER 5th

Hi God,

It's me – Helen. I have a confession to make. For a minute back there I expected to meet you sooner rather than later. Just what happened? I know what occurred physically – I had some kind of seizure as a result of the birth, and I think I nearly died. But spiritually . . . well, I had these wonderful, glorious, technicolour dreams. It was like I was in the Garden of Eden – viewed through the eyes of Alice in Wonderland. However, instead of the Mad Hatter and the Queen of Hearts there were people from my life whom I had lost, all coming to say hello. They were smiling and wanting to hug me, and there were thousands of angels, one of whom was impossibly handsome and I swear looked just like George Clooney!

I saw a massive wall of intense white light and this beautiful radiant smile shining through it and I felt this deep warmth, it was intoxicating . . . and then the next thing I know, I wake up to find Billy and the kids singing and dancing round my bed.

Bizarre doesn't begin to describe it . . . do you think you could, please? You must know what happened. Please let me know. I'm grateful to be alive. SO grateful and so HAPPY to have Liberty Edith. But I need you to fill in the blanks for my own peace of mind. Thank you for saving me.

(Once again) Much love,

Helen xx

OCTOBER 7th

Hello my lovely daughter,

Yes indeed, you're right, you were for a few minutes hovering on the border between life and death. It's a place where, for those who love me, the curtain between time and eternity becomes very thin – not just transparent, but actually porous. So your spirit was able to pass through and see something of the transcendent beauty of eternity. Of course, your memory is also somewhat coloured by the drugs that were coursing through your brain at the time. I'm glad you didn't see the Mad Hatter and the Queen of Hearts – that really would have been a function of the drugs. But those people whom you have loved and lost were allowed to come and see you to encourage you to keep going and not give up. They were a little foretaste of what awaits everyone who enters my eternal home. The family of heaven is immense.

As for the angels, they delight to serve my children. They watch over them from the moment they are born until the moment they pass through the veil into this reality. Each of them has an assignment to look after one of my children. Who knows, yours could even look like George Clooney! My friend and servant, Paul, described me in these words '. . . the Blessed and Undisputed Ruler, High King, High God. He's the only one death can't touch, his light so bright no one can get close.' So that was the wall of intense white light. It was your approach to my presence. What you saw was my smile. I am your proud and loving Dad. As that wrapped around and entered you, I sensed that your inner turmoil was stilled and lots of your hurts began to melt away. It was then that Billy and the kids entered into faith, believing for your healing and you joined in with the song by whispering, 'Oh yeah!' I hope it's not too bizarre, just maybe strange to you at this moment. But it represents reality and it is a promise of all that is to come. I'm glad too that you are alive because there is still so much for you to do. It was a joy to be able to save you. Bless you my daughter. Be at peace and be happy, or – as they used to say in the old days – bless you.

Always and forever, your loving Dad,

GOD

OCTOBER 10th

Dear God,

We've just got back from HMP and seeing Tom. It was hard. Really tough to see him incarcerated like that. But he did appear to be quite calm – which is more than can be said for his mum. Helen was *very* distressed. For the first twenty minutes she barely uttered anything intelligible. Finally, in between sobs, she managed to say, 'Tom I'm so upset to see you in here, and just want you to be with us, but I am also so very proud to see that you're working on stuff and most importantly, exploring your friendship with God. Now tell me all about Lefty.' It turns out that Lefty, the reluctant cell mate, having watched how Tom has dealt with things, and in particular the prisoners who were seeking to pick on him and the corrupt screws turning a blind eye to stuff . . . Well, to put it bluntly he's had a bit of an epiphany. Apparently he said to Tom, 'I wanna call you "Tom the Baptist" from now on, you know, like that geezer in the Bible who came before Jesus did?'

Our son, bless him, has yet to correct him and is quite enjoying his new moniker. Turns out the last person called 'The Baptist' had a propensity for drowning people head first in oil drums. Since Lefty has re-named him, he's had absolutely no trouble at all from anybody. Not a peep. Then, just before we left he seemed to hint that one of the gang leaders was 'giving him the eye'. But he followed that up with, 'I'm probably imagining it, Dad.' Anyway, God, apart from the crying fit in the prison, Helen seems to be back on an even keel and Liberty is delightful . . . Annabel and Jack are all OK. So I guess we should thank you for small mercies, eh? And epic ones too. You never cease to amaze me.

Love,

Billy xxxxxxxx

OCTOBER 12th

Billy, my son,

I'm glad you're amazed. But I have to tell you, you haven't seen anything yet. What I'm planning is going to surprise everybody. Your son's arrival and his decision to trust me is like a small pebble that starts an avalanche. Of course, it was hard for you to see him there, and even more so for Helen. But if you can see what I'm doing in him, you will rejoice. It could never have happened in any other place. Of course, the Lefty story was one of a headlong dive into oblivion. But because of Tom, it's been turned around and he's going to start to fly. Tom the Baptist eh? Now there's a thought! A good one. The famous disciple Thomas was someone who journeyed all the way to India telling people about my Son Jesus and he baptised thousands. Perhaps there's a clue there!

Let me tell you, Billy, your boy is growing into a fine young man. I am very proud of him and so should you be. I'm glad things have settled down in the family, even though you all still miss Tom. When you think about it, that's not just a small mercy is it? You're right, a happy family life is something truly epic. Incidentally, when my Son Jesus was around on the earth, almost everywhere he went, the people were amazed. So get ready! More amazing stuff is on the way.

Your always loving,

Dad

OCTOBER 14th

Dear God,

Thanks for your letter. When you write about Tom you make it sound like he's going to do something wild and extraordinary. As far as I can see he's already done that! But I also know from my own experience that you love to use a rebel heart and turn it around to work for good. To your glory. So as ever I'll trust you and keep watching and waiting. As you know we did find it difficult but I did notice a change in Tom. A new-found confidence . . . and one thing he said has really stayed with me. As I left he told me about the gang leader. Then he simply whispered in my ear. 'I'm not afraid any more, Dad.' That lifted my hopes greatly after Helen's tears . . . So we will try to just watch, wait and pray.

Love,

Billy x

OCTOBER 15th

Dear Billy,

What I say about Tom simply reflects the destiny that I have designed for him and which I want him to grasp with all that wonderful energy he possesses. You already know that anybody who is a combination of you and Helen, and with the spiritual inheritance of Haakon in his life, is going to be wild and extraordinary for me. What seems to have derailed his life, he has given to me and I will use it to get it right on track. You know I will keep on working on him. After all, I am still working on you. So you're right to trust me. Look out for those little signs that I am on the case.

What he said to you as you left was one of those little things that is actually huge. Fear has been an ever-present companion for Tom ever since early childhood. Your absences and Helen's pain generated a huge anxiety in him. This in turn was a fertile seedbed after the trauma of the kidnap. Eddie Fast's face has been in his mind in the years ever since that. Fear makes people do stupid things. What he did with the drugs was completely stupid. It was the product of a wild and untamed fear deep inside him, a fear that told him he could not rely on anybody and a desire to be secure in himself alone – a Big Man. When he got to prison, the fear almost choked him. It was suffocating. In desperation he cried out to me.

Now he has discovered the first lesson of true faith. I, his heavenly Father, am always bigger than anything he faces. It's the foundation, the first building block of everything that is to come. Wild and extraordinary? Yes, indeed! He will make his mother's heart rejoice and he will make you and me very proud. However, there is a long way to go. So, support him with your prayers every day and whenever I bring him to mind. He will come through.

Your Father of never-ending love,

GOD

OCTOBER 16th

Hi God,

It's me – Tom. I'm doing OK. Though things are kind of tense in here. It almost feels like something's brewing. But then, I'm just a new boy, what do I know? Main thing is, Lefty wants to know how to pray. What shall I tell him?

Love,

Tom

PS One of the prison warders has 'come out' to me. No not in that way but as a Christian! Apparently there are three people on the prison staff who are. But he won't tell me their names!

OCTOBER 18th

Hi Tom,

Well done! Tell Lefty it's a great question. One of the most important ones he could ever ask. It shows he's a lot smarter than he thinks. Tell him to talk to me as if I'm the Dad he never had, the Dad he wished he'd had, a Dad who loves him and believes in him, a Dad who stood there at the moment he was born rejoicing, a Dad who has dreams for him and believes in him still. Tell him to talk to me like that. Tell him what you already know. Tell him Jesus is right there with him, unseen but real. Tell him to talk to Jesus, my eternal Son who has accompanied many on the journey that you are now walking. All around the world, there are many who sit in prison cells whose lifeline is this – Jesus is with me.

Some of them suffer because they are being persecuted for my sake, others because, like you, they have tried to fix their own lives with stupid and selfish acts. Tell him not to forget to breathe! Tell him not breathing is fatal; it's what happens to so many people who have stopped relating to me and have become merely religious. The one known as the Holy Spirit is my breath. You are learning to breathe in that presence. It's the breath of life. Others have called it the water of life. Whatever, you need both air and water to live. I was really glad when that warder 'came out' to you as a Christian. Don't worry about the other three. Eventually you will know who they are one way or another. This is only the start. The fact is when you took your life and turned it over to me, I took it from you, mess and all. I'm going to use it in ways which will leave you gobsmacked, give your dad a bit of a surprise and make your mum proud as well. Keep going, my son, even when problems come. Jails are not easy places to live in. But whatever happens, you will get through. I'm with you.

Always your loving, heavenly Dad,

GOD

OCTOBER 20th

Dear God,

I've just had a phone call from the governor of the prison. Some of the real tough nut prisoners have broken out, smashed up their cells and are now sitting on the roof of one of the wings where they are busy ripping up the tiles and throwing them at the police and warders below. Several officers have been hurt, and they're threatening to use water cannon unless everything calms down. Tom and Lefty are nowhere to be seen. The governor called the Prison Fellowship and asked if there was anybody they knew who could possibly help calm the situation down – somebody the inmates might listen to – and my name came up. So he called. He said, 'I know you've done time and now you and your family are Christians. I'm asking you please to pray for an end to the violence and to consider coming down here to help us.' He also mentioned that Tom and Lefty had gone missing. He fears they may have been taken against their will by the rioters. God, I'm just letting you know this because I'm going down there. As an ex-con I figure I might be able to mediate a little. Plus I need to find my son.

Bye for now,

Billy

PS I haven't told anyone else about this. We don't need Helen to have a relapse.

OCTOBER 20th

Dear God,

Billy has just got a phone call from the prison governor. We both picked it up at the same time. I was in our bedroom. He was downstairs in the hall. I heard everything. I am very frightened. However, we've been through trials before – so I'm going to pray that you save Tom and protect him and Billy as they walk in the fiery belly of an angry beast. Relationship with you boils down to one five-letter word: TRUST. So that's what I'm going to do.

Love,

Helen xx

OCTOBER 22nd

Helen, dear daughter.

You astonish me! Rarely in your culture have I found a mother able to trust me, in spite of her fear, in spite of knowing just how bad things can get. Even more, you amaze me with your understanding. Few people are able to express this central principle as simply as you have done. With this saying you have opened the doors of my kingdom power. You have placed Tom in my hands. I will take care of him.

Your truly proud and loving Father,

GOD

OCTOBER 23rd

Dear Billy,

Well done! You're not panicking. But I know deep inside you are really worried. Do you remember the last time we had a call like this about Tom? I said to you then that the angels are already there and so am I. I am with him. Right now, the closest person to him is my Son Jesus. Tom is already talking to me and I am going to use him in a way that will amaze everybody. At this moment, there is not a lot you can do. You won't be able to get in to where Tom is. But I'm already there in the fullness of my nature. I am there as Father, his eternal Dad, just as I am yours. My Son is in there as his big brother, his Saviour, his King. My Holy Spirit is there bringing the fullness of my presence into everywhere Tom goes. Trust me. Trust in my love and don't allow the enemy to fill you with anxiety. If he dares to raise his ugly head, tell him to naff off in the name of Jesus! That should do it.

With you, son, and with your son.

Your heavenly Dad,

GOD

OCTOBER 23rd

URGENT

God, help us. We've been beaten up, dragged up seven flights of stairs and are now being lectured by the leader of this psychotic rabble 'Johnny Two Fingers'. Lefty's unconscious. They cracked him over the head with a skillet from the kitchen. They said they're going to do us both because they saw us praying with one of the prison guards and because we're a 'bunch of dirty Christian slags'.

Help!

Tom

OCTOBER 25th

Hello son,

I know about the beating. Your big brother Jesus went through the same. Right now you're listening to a lot of insane rubbish. Being the man you are, you want to come back with a smart answer – like your dad! Say nothing. Learn from your big brother. Nothing at all. Wait till Johnny Two Fingers (I know the real story of how he got his name!) runs out of steam. Stay silent. Let my peace fill you.

Wait till he asks you why you're not saying anything, then open your mouth, and I will give you the right words. Only say what I tell you to say. Don't try and add more. My Spirit inside you will help you. I know his story and love even him. Try to keep it in your mind. As you speak, look at Johnny's face – at all their faces. Remember I love each one of them. I know their history and the abuse they have suffered. I have a message for each one of them, especially Johnny. Lefty needs to hear it too. Even though he's unconscious, he will get it. Know that I'm with you. Know that my Son, your big brother, is standing right next to you and he defeated all the powers of hell. So while you deal with the humans, he'll be dealing with the spirits of pain, hatred and violence.

I'm proud of you.

GOD

OCTOBER 29th

Dear God,

When I arrived I was taken to the governor's office. I've got to be honest, it was all looking pretty grim. There was a stale-mate for the best part of thirty-six hours, during which I had to let Helen know why I hadn't come home. I have to say when I told her what was going on she was relatively calm but then, apparently, she had listened in on my phone conversa-tion. (Typical!) Fortunately one of our friends from church, Kathy, had seen the late night news and popped round first thing to make sure we were all right. She didn't tell her about the footage showing Tom chained to a drainpipe and Lefty unconscious, thank goodness.

Anyway, what unfolded was nothing short of miraculous. There were riot police on the ground and a helicopter over-head capturing evidence, and the order was about to be given to storm the building. I was stood there looking at my son Tom, a tiny speck on top of the roof, once again taken against his will, and just praying for your divine intervention.

Then I saw the ringleader of the protesters make his way along the ledge with a piece of lead pipe in his hand. He was shouting at Tom and gesticulating wildly – he literally looked like a man possessed. He raised his arm as if to strike Tom but the blow never landed. The piping just seemed to veer off to the side one inch short of Tom's head and then it looked like he just collapsed onto the tiles as if he'd had a massive electric shock or something. He remained motionless – we couldn't see if he was unconscious or what – and then the rest of the protesters started to climb down, leaving Tom and Lefty and their ringleader up there. At the moment we're trying to get the medics up to them both while the protesters are being taken back to their cells. I have to say they all look extremely passive, it's quite eerie. No one can quite believe the change in their attitude. It's weird.

Will write when I know more later.

Love,

Billy x

OCTOBER 31st

Dear son,

Well done for trusting me and staying at the jail throughout the disturbance. You don't know how much you've
changed. Ten years ago, you would have been a complete
wreck. But because you have walked with me, you carry
my presence with you and you release that presence in
each situation you walk into. So, the governor valued your
being there in the office, because you were bringing the
resource of my presence and my calm right into his office,
even while it seemed and felt as though 'all hell was breaking loose'.

When you were looking at Tom, I saw what you felt –
love and pride for him, such as you have never felt before.
Your prayers had immense power as a result. My servant
Paul once wrote, 'Faith works by love.' You were praying,
and your faith empowered by love reached out to protect
Tom. By the way, you were right about the state of the
man who tried to hit Tom. At that moment, he certainly
was 'possessed'. He was at the centre of a massive clash of
spiritual powers – good against evil, love against hate. I
am sure I don't need to explain to you which one of those
sides won! Tom is at a moment in his walk with me when
his faith is pure and childlike. He hasn't yet had it confused
by lots of clever religious arguments or 'real-life' reserva-
tions about my power. So, I was able to pour my power
through him in a way that was unhindered. Your prayers
also contributed to my eternal Son, Jesus, standing there

as Prince of Peace. That's what made the prisoners so calm. Well done, my son.

Your loving Dad in deepest heaven,

GOD

PS Do you remember that love and pride you felt for Tom on the roof? That's just a tiny fraction of what I feel when I look at you. So take a moment. Let the peace and joy of my approval wrap themselves around you.

NOVEMBER 1st

Hi God,

I'm on the hospital wing at the moment. I'm basically OK, just got a touch of hypothermia while we were on the roof. Lefty's in the next bed. He'll be all right, but he's had some stitches in his head where Johnny Two Fingers clonked him, but as you know he's a tough nut. I have to say you never cease to surprise me! I had faith that we were going to be all right even though we'd had a good beating. From which I'm still a bit sore. What I couldn't work out exactly, was when you were (excuse the metaphor here, God) going to send in the cavalry. Why do you always appear to leave it till the last minute to do so?

Anyway, let me regale you with my version of events – what I believe I saw happen – and then perhaps you can give me your divine perspective on things?

We were in a pretty poor state up there; Two Fingers was banging on about what I was in for, you know the dope and all that . . . he had somehow convinced himself that I had a mule bringing some weed in for me, and basically was pissed off I hadn't offered him a cut or even a smoke. But you and I know that's all past now. I've just got to do my time and I'm out. Then he started calling me a ******* hypocrite and said he was going to smash my skull in.

I remember words coming from my lips that weren't from my head: 'Johnny, you can do what you like. But until you can fill that big angry aching hole in your heart, you will never be happy. Trust me.' Well, that stopped him in his tracks. For a second everything changed, I think we all felt it – and there was a moment when I thought it might be over. But then a kind of desperate look came back into his eyes. It was at that point he came at me with the lead pipe. I thought he was going to kill me. But as he brought the pipe down on my head – well, I didn't feel a thing. I closed my eyes and prepared for the pain and when I opened them he was unconscious in the corner by the opposite chimney! Just like he'd been flung there. A limp rag doll. Not only that, big fat tears were coursing down his face. The rest of the rioters immediately seemed to calm down and one of them said, 'How did you do that, Tom? I've never seen anything like that before. And when he came at you . . . it was like you were protected by an invisible force-field.'

I told him the truth. 'I didn't do anything. God did.'

And he turned round to the rest of them and said, 'Did you all see that?' They all quietly nodded their heads. Some of them were openly weeping . . . and then one by one they quietly got up off the roof, took down the barricades they'd erected by the fire exit and filed silently downstairs. It was like all the aggression and hate had been sucked out of them. God, I'd love to know just exactly what you did?

Oh and one final thing, as a result of my involvement in the riot's peaceful outcome, the governor is recommending me for early parole! So, looking forward to hearing from you.

Love,

Tom

NOVEMBER 5th

Tom, my son,

You did brilliantly and I am massively proud of the way you carried yourself through those two days. Do me a favour, tell Lefty that I'm also very pleased with him and proud of him. When he asks you, 'Why would he be proud of me?' you can tell him 'It's because he's your Dad.' He needs to hear that because he never had a dad before. I know you went on believing. That's one of the reasons why I'm proud of you.

You ask why I always appear to leave it until the last minute to 'send in the cavalry'. That's an interesting question. It's very simple, though – if I had intervened at the moment when trouble began to arise, you would never have had a chance to grow in faith or develop courage and, most importantly, grow in understanding that no matter how difficult situations become, I can always carry you through.

You ask for my perspective on your time on the roof. Johnny Two Fingers may be scary to you, but his whole security system relies on others being afraid of him. When that doesn't happen, he gets really scared. That's why he worked himself up to attack you, telling himself all sorts of stories about you bringing in dope and cutting him out of his share. Remember what I told you? Look at him, say nothing, wait till he asks why you're not saying a word, then open your mouth and I will speak through you. And that is what

I did. I opened your eyes to see what was really going on.

In turn, he saw something in you that he has never seen before – my love. It scared him even more and that's why his anger exploded. But your trust in me gave immense power to the angel that stands alongside you at all times. Your dad was praying as well. When the angel stuck out his arm, Johnny's lead pipe was held back and him with it. Why did he have tears coming out of his eyes while he lay there? Because he's never met that sort of tough love before and he met it in you. I warn you now, what happened up there is going to cause a few scratched heads. In your kind of world where the people proudly proclaim they can't believe in anything they can't see or that can't be 'scientifically' proved, angelic interventions are impossible to accept. They will probably make you tell the story several times and they will come up with an explanation to satisfy their unbelief. Don't worry about it. We know what happened!

You asked me how the aggression and hate had been removed from the other protestors. Jesus came. Your utter commitment to him and your active faith released him to stand alongside you as Prince of Peace. The peace he brings is not just the absence of conflict. It is the positive peace of my kingdom and where that comes there is no room for hatred or aggression. It simply cannot function. The men who wept did so because they felt free of terror and rage for the first time in their lives. As I said before, you did brilliantly. Congratulations on being recommended for an early parole. I think you'll find what happens next rather interesting!

Your loving and proud Father in deepest heaven,

GOD

NOVEMBER 30th

Dear God,

Sorry I haven't been in touch – I've been otherwise engaged! Thank you so much for Liberty. She's kept me very busy these past weeks. Still, you're never far from my thoughts. Life seems to be getting back on a more even keel now and we have the wonderful news that, as promised, as a result of Tom's involvement in ending the riot the prisoner governor has got permission to release him as long as he wears his electronic tag for the next year and agrees to see his parole officer once a week. His pal Lefty is also due out soon.

It turns out that the pair of them want to go to what Tom calls 'vicar college', and then work with young offenders in prisons. Funny how our mess sometimes becomes our message . . .

Billy and I are still living off the high of how things have worked out, very much in love, he seems to be growing ever more tender and thoughtful with me. Having been through so much together I guess we're becoming firm believers in the old adage, 'What doesn't kill you, makes you stronger' – that and the knowledge that no matter how high we climb or how hard we fall you are always there, everlasting and constant in your love for us.

Thank you.

Much love,

Helen xx

PS I promise I won't leave it so long before writing again – and oh yes, my dad and sister are flying in from Canada for Christmas – we'll all be together again for the first time in ages! REALLY looking forward to it . . .

DECEMBER 1st

My beautiful daughter,

Do you think I don't know how busy you have been? What I most enjoy about you is the touch of thought that you constantly bring to our relationship. Your thoughts go to all kinds of matters throughout the day. But they always return to me and I am always aware of you.

It is wonderful news that Tom is going to be released early from the prison. Just bear in mind, he's very much like his father and because he is so like Billy, he may well find what you call 'vicar college' rather testing! Lefty also has much to learn and to grow through before he's ready for anything like that. But they are both right to dream. I have great plans for them. I've been delighted to watch Billy as he has grown more tender and thoughtful. It's wonderful to see. You mention the old saying 'What doesn't kill you makes you stronger'. That is true as long as you give what tries to kill you to me. Sadly, sometimes what doesn't kill people makes them more bitter. I don't want that to happen to you. You are right, of course, I am always here for you, everlasting in nature and constant in love.

Finally, I am so thrilled to know that this Christmas is going to be truly a family Christmas with your dad and your sister coming in from Canada. I hope you sense my smile beaming down upon you all.

All of heaven's love.

Your everlasting Dad,

GOD

DECEMBER 4TH

Dear God,

I can't quite believe it, but this Christmas, for the very first time, we're all going to be together. Sara and Haakon are flying in from Toronto and my son Victor is coming from New York where he now works as a journalist with the *New York Times*. I am so proud of him. And to cap it all, Tom is set to be released on Christmas Eve! Helen is beside herself with all the excitement . . . So there'll be me and Helen, Tom, Annabel, Jack, Liberty, Victor, Sara and Haakon all round our big dining table. I can't wait!

Love,

Billy x

DECEMBER 23rd

Dear Billy,

This Christmas is a special gift for you and for the whole family. It's one of those moments in life where the beautiful, surprising and glorious reality of heaven shines on my earthly family and you gain just a tiny foretaste of what the heavenly party will really be like – so, enjoy! When you look round that table, reflect on this – it's all come together because I am a God who loves to do beautiful things for people, things they do not deserve. You won't be the only one smiling!

Always your loving Dad,

GOD

DECEMBER 30th

Dear God,

Well, that has to have been the best Christmas yet. Tom was released from the prison at midday on Christmas Eve and it was remarkable what happened. The governor put on his report that not only had he been a model prisoner, but the effect he and Lefty had after the riot was to 'bring an almost supernatural sense of order and calm to the place'.

I laughed and cried together when he ran out of the prison gates. Sometimes those two emotions can be very closely linked. Haakon, Sara and Victor arrived later in the day and Tom and I picked them up from the airport. We had a very different journey back to our house compared to last time. Thank you, God! Haakon is not surprisingly looking older and, if I'm honest, moving slower, but then he is eighty years old now. Sara was as calm, classy and elegant as ever, and as for Victor, he's just been awarded a prize for his 'commitment to investigative and narrative journalism'. Well he always was a seeker after truth!

He had found out that just before the stock market crash, two senators had got wind of what was happening, withheld the information until they had divested themselves of their financial portfolios and been paid out, and then leaked it through a third party. So they played a key part in bringing America to its knees. So it was our Victor who exposed the corruption. But you know all that – after all, you see right inside every man's heart. And even though you knew already I just had to tell you myself. He's my boy, you see. Annabel and Jack were overjoyed to see Tom home, and now they're both a little older we have now explained the full story of what happened to their big brother.

They were overwhelmed just with that, I think, but then Tom also explained about his faith and just how that had radically impacted him. I'm hoping they will learn from his example and not go down the same painful road. By the way, he absolutely adores Liberty. That's his sister, I mean, although I also know he loves being free as well! And as for my beautiful wife Helen – well this Christmas I bought her a new platinum eternity ring; I think I love her more than ever. She is like a fine wine that gets better through the years – full bodied, with a delicate bouquet and best savoured slowly after being laid down!

Thank you God for all you've done and continue to do for me.

Love,

Billy xxx

NEW YEAR'S DAY

My beloved son,

I agree with your assessment. Looking back over your life, that *was* the best Christmas yet. For Tom, it marks the moment he crossed over into a new land of considered life-purpose, of destiny. Do you know what Jewish people do every year? On the Passover night, they hold a special meal at which the youngest child asks, 'What makes this night different from all other nights?' Then they tell the story of the night I delivered them out of slavery in Egypt. They walked through waters that threatened death. But that journey set them free to walk into a life of liberty. For thousands of years, my ancient people have faithfully kept that feast.

This Christmas has been a glorious celebration of deliverance. Treasure it. Bank it for the future. Every year at Christmas, tell the story again. Remember it together. Remembering is the opposite of dismembering. It's putting it all back together so that it's as real in the present as it was the first time. Why do I advise you to bank it? Because the Enemy hates you and all that has been accomplished in your life. He will strike back. He will do all he can to rob you of the joy you now know. You mentioned the emotions of laughter and tears being closely linked. You are right. In a fallen world – where there is so much evil, hatred, venom and suffering – love, joy, health, happiness and laughter have to march beside the tears. To live the life of my kingdom in a world the Enemy claims as his own territory is to declare war against evil. At some point evil will strike back. Consider what Jesus endured at the cross. Suffering and glory go hand in hand. So, treasure these special days. Look at Haakon. Understand the pain and tragedy he has walked through and the serenity and joy you now see. It is what I plan to do for you. It's great that Victor has inherited your entrepreneurial spirit and used it to such good effect. He is a fine legacy for you. Rejoice in him.

Well done for sitting down with Annabel and Jack to explain what happened to Tom. Almost certainly you will have saved them from going down the same painful road – though they will make their own mistakes! I love the idea of the eternity ring you bought Helen – fitting, because you two are building an inheritance that will resonate in eternity. I enjoyed the description of her as a fine wine, though I'm not sure she'll relish being described as 'full-bodied'. However, your allusion to love-making is almost worthy of Solomon. His Song contains many such pictures. Continue to enjoy all the bounty that is being poured out on you. It comes with my undivided love.

Your Father in heaven,

GOD

JANUARY 4TH

My dear Billy,

I had to write and say thank you for a wonderful Christmas. It was lovely to all be together again and to meet Liberty for the first time. She has her mother's beautiful green eyes and your cheeky smile!

There is something I need to let you know, though, that I feel is better written down than said face to face. You see, Billy, I'm dying . . . Sara and Victor don't know yet, and neither does Thor, as I've managed to disguise the symptoms pretty well . . . but the fact is that I have two aggressive cancers growing quite rapidly – one in my pancreas and the other in my liver. The doctors have been very kind and have given me the option of throwing some chemo at it, but the truth is I've seen first hand what that does to people and I'd rather maintain a good quality of life without my body having to wrestle with a bombardment of cytotoxic drugs. I'm ready to meet my Maker any time he wants – what I don't want is a long drawn out demise. So I'm praying he will take me quickly.

I need your help though – and your promise that you will always look after Victor and Sara. You know you will lose me but I have to lose all of you. That seems so unfair when we've only got to know each other in the past couple of years. Still, I would rather have had that precious time with you and see Victor, Sara and everybody so beautifully reconciled than never to have had a glimpse of God's gracious hand in such loving action. I only hope he will be kind to me and take me home before life gets too painful. I know this is a difficult letter to receive, but I also know you are faithful and will consider carefully what I have asked and will know when to share that with Helen and the rest of the family. I would ask for your prayers please, as this weekend Sara, Victor and Thor are all coming home for my eighty-first birthday. It will be a painful time for us all.

Billy, you have come so far and God answered my prayers for your life. But I never would have thought you would become so truly my son in God. He is so good. I hope he will now answer my prayers – just one more time.

With the Father's love,

Haakon x

JANUARY 6TH

Dear Haakon,

I don't know what to say. All I know is I have to write something. You've become my earthly dad, the only true one I ever had. It's because of you that I've learnt to really know and love our heavenly Dad. To lose you so quickly tears me apart. I was such a scumbag when you first knew me and you have shown me the kind of love I have no right to expect. I understand your choice about the drugs. But I hate the idea that it means you're going to leave us sooner rather than later. You want my help and of course you have it.

Whatever you want me to do, I will do. I will certainly always take care of Victor and Sara. Whatever is needed – anything! Nothing is so encouraging to me as the fact that you trust me with them and then you write and tell me 'I also know you are faithful'. I pray I manage to get to the point of being as faithful as you. Of course I will be praying that God will grant your final prayer. I remember we once had a conversation about this kind of thing. You told me that your ambition was to die well – if possible, well in body, but whatever, to die well in spirit. It looks as though your first prayer will not be answered. But I pray that your second one will be. I want to see you again before you go. I'll be talking to Helen to see whether we should come together. Thank you for all you have been to me and still are. Thanks again for all the undeserved love you have shown me.

Your loving son,

Billy

Haakon, my son,

Billy showed me the letter you wrote to him. It was wise and generous. He doesn't really understand what you have done in trusting him with the news of your cancer even before you talk to Thor, Sara and Victor. In asking him to always be there to look after Victor and Sara, you have entrusted the most precious things you have to him. Well done.

I'm glad that you and Thor are closer now. I will be watching over him. When you wrote to Billy, you said you were losing them all. That could not be further from the truth. You have them in your heart. Do you think you will not carry them with you in your heart into my heavenly home? Do you think that I, the true and only Father of all things, would not understand the heart of a father who wants to know how his children are? Your view of them will be very different when you finally step into my eternal home.

Here's my promise to you in answer to the prayer you have articulated so clearly to Billy: I will walk with you every step of the way and I will draw closer to you the nearer you get to the gates of the beautiful city. I know you remember the promise my Son made, 'I will never leave you, nor forsake you.' He speaks for me. I will be there. I will walk with you through it all. My Son and I together will carry the burden with you. I know the road will be difficult at times but I am so looking forward to seeing you, my dear son, stepping through the gates of the celestial city. We have quite a welcome planned for you.

Your ever-loving Father in deepest, highest and widest heaven,

GOD

Dear Dad,

This is the toughest letter I've ever had to write to you. You are my heavenly Dad. But the truth is I don't think I ever would have properly got to know you without the one who became my earthly dad. At least the nearest thing to a dad I ever had on this planet. Now, after knowing him for such a short time, just a few years, I'm going to lose him. We're all going to. The family are going to lose their beloved granddad.

Why? Haakon's such a good man. Why should he suffer the kind of pain he's facing? It's all wrong. He's gentle and kind, the godliest man I've ever known. I know you love him and I'm sure you've got great things planned for him in the heavenly home. But I want to know why he has to go now? Why in such a painful way? We love him so much. In some ways, it's like he's become the heart of the family and now we're going to lose him. Everything inside me is screaming. But I want to do this right. I know you can heal. Your Son Jesus did such amazing miracles when he was on earth and I know he's done thousands of them since then through people in the church. Yet when I start to pray that you will heal him, it feels to me as if you're saying, 'Not this time.' I understand. We all have to go sometime. Perhaps it really is his time to go. But the pain in my heart is almost unbearable.

So, I'm praying, if you're not going to heal him, then answer his prayer that he will not suffer too much pain. Above all, let him know your presence every step of the way. He is your

143

man and your son, as well as the man I'm so proud to call my dad. So, I give him to you. I'm really glad Jesus made it clear there's no such thing as death in the heavenly realm. So we will meet again.

I trust you, heavenly Dad, and I trust you with my earthly dad, Haakon Fredrickson.

Your loving son,

Billy x

JANUARY 11th

Billy, my dearly loved son,

I know only too well how much Haakon's letter has shaken you. Well done for responding the way you have. I'm truly proud. Before I answer your question, let me ask you one. Do you understand what he has done in writing to tell you about the cancer before even telling Sara, Victor or Thor? He has given to you his place of spiritual leadership. In asking you to look after Sara and Victor, he has recognised in you the seeds of fatherhood. When he wrote 'I also know you are faithful,' he was telling you he has seen some of my own character showing through you. It's partly an inheritance from him. The prayers of his faithfulness and covenant love for you have borne fruit.

You don't know what a joy it is for him to be able to write to you and entrust you with the family, as if to an eldest son. He hasn't given up on Thor, and he won't. But at this moment he knows he can trust you with them and that is an enormous comfort to him. You're right; he has become a gentle and kind man. But he also lived many years in deceit, unable to tell the story of his time in London. Essentially a man of integrity, nonetheless he lived a lie. It wounded him deeply inside. He had to maintain such control, hard on himself and hard on others. When humans behave like that, they have no idea of what they are doing to their whole being.

In his death, my Son paid for all the consequences of sin – winning freedom from guilt and healing of sickness.

...n who came to Jesus for healing went ...eceiving it. That is our heart. But this ...complex in a world where you as a race ...atan so much authority. In the war between ...d hell, sickness is one of his most powerful ...s. Yet at times he overreaches himself – and I allow ...do so. You see, sometimes, in the extremity of pain, men abandon their pride and find their way home to me. Others firmly trust me as they face this kind of test, boldly believing in my grace and in the healing victory of the cross up to the very moment when they step through the doors of eternity. Haakon is one of my choicest saints. I will answer his prayer. When he steps through the gates into my city, he will receive a hero's welcome. His story is not your story. Trust me with him as you trust me with yourself. Your pathway into eternal glory will not be the same as his. But your destination is the same. As you pray for him, entrust him to me. I am his Dad just as much as I am yours. I will be good to him.

Your ever-loving heavenly Dad,

GOD

JANUARY 12th

Dear God,

I am encouraged by all that you have planned for Haakon – it's just that we have to lose him and that will be *very* hard. He has been the best earthly model to me of your perfect love, and now it's as if he's passing the baton to me, along with your blessing, and I am just not sure I can be worthy of that. I know I have the conviction that with you anything is possible. But the thing is, God, sometimes life just feels so brutal. So short. If only I knew as a young man what I know now as I enter my late middle age. I might have taken a different road. You mention my pathway to glory being different from Haakon's . . . I hope so. I wouldn't want to die of cancer, and I certainly don't want to die yet . . .

I spoke to Sara and Victor last night and although they're both obviously distressed they are committed to loving Haakon through your veil of love into eternity. They can see the bigger picture and are doing their very best to look after him, but on a day-to-day basis they are struggling with the evidence of his deterioration. On a video-call it's clear he's looking emaciated. Effectively he's on a liquid diet of nutrients, and he has an IV drip in his arm dispensing glucose so his blood sugars remain constant. He can still make it to the bathroom with help, but it takes him about ten minutes and when he sleeps, which is often, his breathing is regulated by oxygen tanks by the side of his bed.

Helen's friendship with Sara is proving very important and they email each other back and forth all the time – and I'm in

...Victor. He mentioned that he might like
...d work in England but, for the time being,
...o stay out there for his grandfather and mum.
...e did come over but also know I mustn't pres-
...Especially at the moment.

...doing well and hasn't missed one of his appoint-
...Thank goodness he'd done enough A-level papers
already to pass them at least before all the drugs stuff blew
up. So it looks like he'll be able to enrol at theological college
this coming September. Jack is playing football for his school
team and there's been the odd comment about him going to
one of the football academies. Annabel has started painting
using acrylics and has created some, um, extraordinary crea-
tions. She says to me, 'Dad I just pray and paint and then see
what happens.'

As for Liberty, she is crawling round the lounge at a rapid
pace. I think she's going to be quite a handful. So overall life
is good! I'll be in touch soon.

Love,

Billy x

FEBRUARY 1st

Dear Billy,

One of the things I do love about you is your capacity to bounce back. You write with such feeling of Haakon's fight with cancer. You are able to picture so much of it because you've seen it before in your mother's story. But I hope you can see that you must not read into Haakon's story your mother's pain, alienation and suffering. Though I met her at the end, I am walking with Haakon through this right now. I'm impressed that in spite of all that, when you come to describing life in the family at the moment, your conclusion is that life is good.

You're right, Tom really is doing very well and I continue to have my eye on Lefty! Keep praying for him. He is enjoying living for me at the moment, but theological college will be more testing than he realises. As you know, Jack's dreams are the dreams of so many, to be in a team playing in the Premiership and scoring the winning goal in the cup final. Those are big dreams and the bling around them can blind young men to the fact that though they are big dreams, they are also quite shallow ones and have a limited lifespan. A full life needs more than the blazing rise and fall of a football career to sustain it. Your prayers and my dreams for Jack are about more. Above all, I want him to be an adventurer for me.

Eric Liddell won Olympic gold and permanent glory for himself, but his greatest achievements were his years in China, working to establish what is now one of the most vibrant churches in the world. His death in a prisoner of war camp crowned the glory of his life and sealed his status as one of Scotland's greatest heroes. More importantly, he is one of heaven's heroes.

Annabel makes me laugh. I see her in the studio, her overalls covered in paint, paint in her hair and across her face. She is completely unconscious of it all, focussed only on the canvas in front of her. She is wonderfully extraordinary and all the more beautiful for being completely unaware of it.

And then of course, Liberty – you already know from her response to music that she is a dancer. Wait until you hear her sing. I think she'll be a handful. But would you want it any other way?

So, we return to Haakon. You say that he has been the best earthly model of my love. He has done well. You say he's passing the baton to you along with my blessing and you're right. Think about that. Beware of the 'if only'. Don't try to rewrite your history. It is what it is. I work with what is, not with what might have been. Now we are at the point where the baton changes hands. What's the secret of doing that successfully? Timing. What's the reason it goes wrong so frequently? Timing. I brought Haakon into your life at exactly the right moment. I have allowed him just the right amount of time to create in you a beautiful crystalline seed of fatherhood. Because of you, his last few years have been years of freedom and joy such as he never knew before. Now he is nearing the gates to my eternal home. He has journeyed well and lived a full life. Now his face is shining with the light that beams upon him from his eternal home. And you, my dear son, are ready. This is the moment when the baton changes hands. You're in the right place at the right time. The timing is perfect. Rejoice for his victory even as you weep for the loss of his presence. It is – as one of your best writers once said, leaving a funeral service – just for a while. Be at rest in your heart. This is the right time.

Your loving, eternal Father,

GOD

FEBRUARY 13th

From: victor.fidget@newshound.com
To: billy.fidget@thefidgets.com

Dear Billy/Dad,

It's time for you to come and say goodbye to Grandpa. He's getting weaker by the day and the doctor reckons he might not last the week. Come soon. We need you.

Love,

Victor x

FEBRUARY 13th

From: billy.fidget@thefidgets.com
To: victor.fidget@newshound.com

Son, I'm on my way. I've been on the internet and got us tickets to Toronto so we'll be with you in 24 hours. Tell Haakon I'm coming for the handover of the baton. He'll understand.
  Love you son,

  Dad/Billy

FEBRUARY 19th

Dear God,

Just got back from Toronto having said goodbye to Haakon. I was shocked when I got there, to see this very vital man reduced to a bag of bones. His skin was sallow and jaundiced and his face was bloated from the steroids, with his breathing regulated by a machine. There was a team of nurses on eight-hour shifts looking after him at home, and that morning the doctor had come early and told the family Haakon would most likely die that day. Helen and I got to the house at lunch-time, and were met at the door by Thor, who greeted us warmly, and were then taken upstairs to see my old friend. Sara and Victor were sitting by the bed monitoring his every breath, but after a couple of minutes all together Sara said, 'I'll leave you and Dad alone for a moment,' and she took Helen downstairs with Victor. Haakon waved at me to come closer to him and whispered, 'I love you like my son. Just three things in life . . . three . . . love, loss and trust . . .', then his bony little hand gripped mine fleetingly with such brief intensity, and then let go just as quickly and I could see him slipping away and I called out, 'Come now!' and everyone burst into the room, to grab one last little piece of this great man for one final time, and then he was gone. I almost thought I saw his spirit leave his body.

We were all sobbing, Thor most of all – he kept looking at his father and saying, 'Dad, I'm so sorry . . . so sorry.' Victor was calm and just had a constant stream of tears flowing down his face; other than that he said nothing. Helen and

Sara clung to each other, joined in the grief of two sisters, and I . . . I just held him, stroking his forehead, still warm but his soul had gone. The one man who demonstrated to me better than anyone else in this life what it was and is to be a man of God. My rock. My safe place, to whom I could talk about anything. Gone. The man who had prayed for my salvation and brought up my son as his own. A man who never owned hate. A man who had the ability to look at everything and everyone differently. My spiritual father. And his last words are seared deep into my heart. *Love* – I shall love as if every day is my last on this earth. *Loss* – I am now beginning to learn just how painful that is. And to comfort those who mourn. *Trust* – in God, for everything. I will not waste these words.

Love,

Billy xxxx

FEBRUARY 21st

My son,

You have grown so much. It was truly important that you and Helen were there at the end for Haakon. On a human level, it meant so much to him. It was truly significant. Although he was terribly diminished by that horrible disease, as he prepared for his departure he knew that you were crossing the Atlantic just to be with him for the moment he crossed the finish line. It was gloriously affirming.

Didn't you think it was remarkable that the person who came to meet you at the door was Thor? His heart has softened so much. It was right that they left you alone with Haakon for a few moments. He called you to him to pass on the baton, like he said. When he had done that, he felt free to leave the life of your world in obedience to the call from heaven.

It's important that you go on praying for Thor. He is a lonely man. Stand ready to be an older brother, almost like a father to him. He will need you and in time he will need your forgiveness just as you need to hear him speak his forgiveness to you.

Victor, of course, has lost the one who brought him up and this will dramatically change his relationship with you. Be ready. Some of what flows from this will be painful to pass through, but immeasurably healing. Now the legacy of Haakon has passed to you. You called him 'My rock, My safe place.' Remember where he got that from.

David wrote it years ago: 'The LORD is my Rock, my Fortress.' Just as Haakon's death has changed earthly relationships, it will change our relationship too. Haakon exercised the role every father is supposed to perform. He created in you a dad-shaped space, a space for me to be more truly and more closely your Dad than you've ever known. His last words were born of long years walking with me through pain and joy, triumph and sorrow. There is much wisdom celebrated in them: love, loss, trust.

I've said it to you before and I'll say it again, 'You're a lucky man, Billy Fidget.'

Always your loving Dad,

GOD

SUNDAY NIGHT

Billy, my dear son,

There is so much I wanted to say. I thought I should put it down in writing, because I think, by the time you arrive, I will be too weak to say very much. So I have written this for you to read after I am gone, and I will post it to you, so you are reminded that even when you think that's it, that's the end – it won't be. I know in novels, this kind of letter usually begins By the time you read this, I'll be dead . . . *Actually, of course, the glorious truth is that by the time you read this, I will be more alive than I've ever been. Just think, Billy, I am going to see Jesus face to face. Then he will escort me into the presence of his Father, there to see our heavenly Dad, to see his smile full on. Won't that be amazing?*

You know, I prayed that I would not have to suffer pain on this journey. The truth is there has been lots of pain and at times it has felt almost unbearable. Yet I have known the presence of Jesus closer and more real than ever in my life before. People talk about intimacy. But it's nothing compared to what I have known these last few weeks. Our God is so amazing. There are moments now when the veil between heaven and earth seems almost like a mist, like one of those diaphanous curtains that drift in the slightest breeze.

So, although I know you will weep for me because we will not see each other face to face in this world again, I ask you also to rejoice for what I will be seeing even when you read this. Already there are moments when I sense heaven drawing near and the joy is almost close enough to touch. I'm going to rest now. I will carry on tomorrow.

TUESDAY MORNING

I couldn't work on this yesterday. I was too weak. But I have to tell you this, last night in my dreams I saw it, Billy, I saw it – heaven, more beautiful than anything I've ever seen or dreamed of. Just amazing. I know we live in the kind of world where people will tell you 'it's just the influence of the drugs' or 'it's the compensating mechanism of his brain as it begins to shut down'. It's all nonsense! They can prattle away as much as they like, but I've seen it and I know where I'm going. So Billy, never give up hope. You will face difficult times. Before we meet again, you will go through heartbreak. But as he's been with me, Jesus will walk beside you and he will bring you through. He's like that.

LATER THAT DAY

I have to tell you this.

When I look back I am amazed at what God has done. The days when I hated you and wished you dead are like a distant memory of an old nightmare. I can scarcely believe that was me or that I felt that way. Somehow God has taken what you did to Sara, redeemed it and covered it with glory. What an extraordinary story I have lived through! Incredibly, you have become one of the most precious parts of it. You know I forgave you for what you did to Sara. But there are still days when you listen to the voice of the accuser. So, see this written down Billy. Believe it once and for all, Sara and I forgive you totally for what you did to her.

There is no tiny lurking shadow of anything other than joy and love in our hearts. We have forgiven you totally and accepted you unreservedly.

Thor, obviously, is not yet at that point. But he is softening. Now my prayers for him will be made from another place. So I ask you to take up that charge. Pray for Thor until he comes through to full knowledge of Jesus and the Father's love for him. I ask you to do this because in becoming my son as you have, you have inherited a brother. I know, as I wrote before, that you are faithful. In this, I am certain you will not fail.

I cannot tell you what a joy it has been for me to see my beautiful daughter, Helen, and watch her grow into the radiant beauty that has become hers. As for my new grandchildren (they still feel new to me) – how I love them; Tom with that mischievous twinkle in his eye. I think he'll make a great minister of God! Jack, the fierce competitor. I look at you and see where he got that from. And oh my beautiful Annabel, is there a love that tears more at the heart of a man than the love he feels for his granddaughter? If there is, I have never come across it. I wanted to be there for the day of her wedding. But I know I'll never do that now. Maybe the Father himself will let me see! Who knows! And tiny Liberty, what little I've seen of her, wriggling in her mother's arms – Helen is such a great mum, isn't she? I suspect she is going to give you lots of sleepless nights for all kinds of reasons.

MIDNIGHT

So my son, this is it. These are the last words I will express to you this side of the gates of heaven. Get your priorities right. So much has happened to you recently, I think you've put the issue

160

of your destiny on the back burner. But I haven't forgotten what you told me the heavenly Father said, about the call to 'the impossible dream'. Don't drop that. Think about it and pray. God still has something special for you to do. You've become to me even more than a son, you've been a friend, almost like the young brother I never had. In your weeping don't suffer too much. I am off to the best place. All that I've handed over to you, I do with joy, and huge gratitude to my heavenly Father. I know you will not fail. Your loving earthly dad,

  Haakon Friedriksen

PS They've just told me you'll be here tomorrow midday. I'll wait. Dad

AUGUST 12th

Dear God,

Six months have passed since Haakon went to be with you, and there is not one day when I don't think about him. I keep his last letter to me inside my Bible, and read it every day. It contains such profound wisdom. If I can achieve just one iota of that wisdom while I draw breath then I will die a happy man. Not that I'm in any hurry, mind you! I'm still earning my living selling cars, but I haven't forgotten 'the impossible dream'. It was almost the last thing Haakon wrote to me. Maybe cars could be part of it. I've always loved them and I'm good at trading in them. Maybe that's the way forward? Tell me what you think.

I now pray (as you suggested) every day for Sara, Victor and Thor along with everyone else, and there have been some interesting results. Victor has got a job with the *Daily Telegraph* and is set to move over here just before the summer holidays start, and Sara thinks she has found the man she's going to spend the rest of her life with. His name is Conan. I had to laugh. I immediately thought of that film, *Conan the Barbarian*. Victor tells me his mum is head over heels, but he doesn't like him very much. Describes him as 'shifty' and he's concerned that he's playing fast and loose with his mother's affections. But then, I don't suppose any son will take to his mother finding new love easily. Thor has taken to emailing me and has asked for my advice on a work problem he has. Significantly, his first email to me was an apology for having given me such a hard time back in the day. It was really lovely, as I got to give some of the grace back to him that Haakon had so kindly invested in me. Something is definitely changing the shape of his heart, and I think maybe it is you!

By the way, Liberty has started toddling and the other day managed to 'post' a digestive biscuit into the DVD player. When we took it to be repaired they also found a hair clip, a plectrum and three peanuts! No wonder the blasted thing didn't work!

Will write again soon.

Love,

Billy x

PS Helen sends her love.

AUGUST 13th

Billy, my dear son,

I am not surprised that you continue thinking about
Haakon. His love for you was quite extraordinary by
human standards, and a joy to me because it so deeply
reflected my own love for you.

You suggested that if you can *achieve just one small iota
of his wisdom while you live, then you can die a happy
man.* I think it's a bit soon to be talking about that! You
already reflect some of the wisdom he imparted to you
and more which, believe it or not, you have learned
through your walk with me. But your race is not finished
yet. You're not even in the final straight.

I'm glad you're praying every day for Sara, Victor and
Thor. There are bound to be interesting results. People
might call them mere coincidences. But then as one wise
man said: 'When I pray, coincidences happen and when I
don't – they don't!'

It's great that Victor got that job with the *Daily Telegraph*.
You'll enjoy seeing him and your kids will benefit enor-
mously from having their big brother near. Keep praying
for Sara. Since Haakon died she has been lonely and it is
not surprising that she is drawn to Conan. He is a charm-
ing and plausible man. I won't say more than that, except
that Victor is quite perceptive!

Your relationship with Thor is really important. I felt
for him above all when his father died. The tears that
flowed were not just grief. They were an expression of

his longing for the relationship he turned his back on for so long. The stupid thing is that he knew all the time, in turning away from his father because his father was willing to forgive you, he was wounding himself more than anyone else. Sadly, the pain he felt was precious to him as a weapon with which to punish his father – too much so for him to give way to his understanding of the damage it did to him. But, following his father's death, he is coming to a place of true repentance.

His email apology was the first step in a link that will enable the relationship with his father to be repaired at last. So keep on giving him lots of the grace that Haakon gave to you. Obviously, you're right – the person who is changing the shape of his heart is Jesus. He always does that when people finally let him in. Keep on praying and stay open to him. That bond is going to be of enormous importance to the whole family.

You don't mention Tom, but I know he is doing well at the moment. His ongoing care for Lefty has made me very proud. And Annabel's canvases are even more amazing than ever. But let's talk about Liberty. You've discovered that her relationship with modern technology is quite creative – but then I think you'll find that will be her approach to life. Whatever else it is, life with Liberty is never going to be dull! She is a combination of the feistiest bits of Helen and the sparkiest bits of you. Rejoice . . . and tremble! You mention that Helen sends her love. In return, I send her the adoring love of her true Dad.

Blessings to both of you from your eternal home and your loving Father,

GOD

PS You tiptoe around 'the impossible dream', but my destiny for people is not always something difficult and horrible. In fact, it is almost invariably linked to something about which they have a passion. I take that passion, once it's surrendered to me, and remake it into a calling. So, if you think it through, something to do with cars might well be right for you! From your fond Father, God.

AUGUST 21st

Phone call:

Tom: Dad, it's Mum! She's gone!
Billy: What do you mean?
Tom: She was pushing Liberty along in the buggy and a car just came round the corner and hit her!
Billy: Where are you?
Tom: On the way to the hospital, in the ambulance.
Billy: I'm coming. See you there.

AUGUST 21st

God,

I'm going to the hospital now. Help us, God!

Billy

AUGUST 21st

Son,

I'm already here.

Dad

EVENING OF AUGUST 21st

Jesus! God!

What have you done? Taken the love of my life just as everything is turning out good! Left the children motherless. And Liberty just eighteen months old? It cannot be possible that you allowed this, after all you're ALL-POWERFUL. So I have to presume everything you have ever told me is complete and utter bullshit. JESUS – THE GREAT PRETENDER. What was it he said on the cross? 'It is finished.' IT IS NOW.

Billy

AUGUST 21st

Billy, beloved brother,

It's me – Jesus. That's the first time you've called out to
me directly since you were drowning in darkness at the
hospital years ago. You ask what we have done. Do you
really think the heavenly Father loves Helen any less than
you? Or the children? My heart was broken at the tomb
of Lazarus – and I was just about to raise him from the
dead! Do you think I don't feel the pain you and the
others feel at a death like this? Did I take her? No. Did the
Holy Spirit kill her? No. He is the Spirit of life. Death is
an affront to us. You have forgotten about the prince of
darkness. Our enemy. Satan. Yes – we together bring light
and life into this world – but it is a constant battle. He
hates all humans with a passionate fire because he hates
us, the three-in-one God. Each of you reminds him of us.

There's a war going on, Billy. You and the whole human
race are in the middle of it. He is the devil, not any kind of
gentleman. With him, there is no honour or 'civilised
warfare'. He fights dirty. He uses anything and everything
to hurt and destroy because he is a user, a defiler of all that
is good. You are walking through the Valley of the Shadow
of Death – but we will not leave you there alone. Do you
remember those three words Haakon gave you at the end?
Love, Loss, Trust. We allowed him to warn you, my dear
brother, of what was coming . . . In all this, our heart is
towards you, planning only good for you and the children,
even Liberty at just one year old. Do you think we don't

feel this injustice? You are my brother and I believe you can rise above this. I don't mind your rage or the bitterness of your heart at the moment. But don't let it take over.

We warned you that he hated you. He is at war with us and with you. After years of nurturing and training, you and Helen had advanced through the ranks until you were both on the frontline. Satan, knowing how much you love Helen, has come after you through her. You are a target-rich environment. He is not subtle and will always come at you where you are most vulnerable. He hopes that by ending Helen's life, he will destroy you. This life is a battle-ground. You know that. But Helen's death was swift, merciful and selfless. Liberty lives because of her last determined thought to protect her daughter. Her very last act in your world ensured that her daughter would live. A very wise man once said, 'The greatest test of his followers is the moment when they perceive God has betrayed them.' This is where you are.

Now it's time to make a stand. You won't find the strength you need in a bottle. But you will find it in me. Tom still believes you're a hero. Stand up and show him what heroes are made of – courage in the face of disaster, faith instead of despair. You described us as 'all-powerful'. All power does come from us, the three-in-one God. But it's not all that matters. We are also all-loving. Relationship is at our heart. If the kingdom of God was simply about the ruthless exercise of power, then Satan's 'kingdom' would have been destroyed in eternity before the world was created. But in order to do it, we would have had to destroy someone accusing us of lust for power, its possession and use without truth or justice. We would have been validating the charge he raised against us. For me and the Father to be who you know us to be, we have to be not only all-powerful, but also all-loving and totally just.

I repeat – you live in a war zone. Here we see and experience things that beggar belief. But I'm your big Brother. I know what is in you. We share the same DNA. I know you can rise above this. You accuse me of being 'the Great Pretender'. Do you really think that as I hung in agony on that cross, and screamed, 'My God, my God, why have you abandoned me?' that I was pretending? When I prayed, 'Father forgive them, they don't know what they're doing,' was I acting? Deep inside, you know I wasn't. And when I said, 'It is finished,' I was not referring to the war between heaven and earth, but to the price that had been paid for the ultimate victory.

Do you see it? I had to prove my heart is love – pure undiluted, unselfish, passionate love. That's the truth. My love is the most powerful force in the whole creation. I love you, my brother and my friend. Through the years, you know I have walked alongside you and upheld you on many occasions. Do not defile Helen's memory and final act by debasing yourself and writhing in bitterness. You all deserve so much better than that. Please trust me now with the agony you feel. I've never failed you yet and I never will.

Your loving Brother, and Friend forever,

Jesus

AUGUST 21st

Billy, my son,

You've already heard from your elder brother, Jesus, and you know our heart towards you is nothing but love. We've allowed you to go through the Valley of the Shadow of Death. Haakon gave you those three words. Of all the men in your life, would he have left you with nothing but a trite line of overblown poetry? Love, Loss, Trust. Quiet your spirit for a moment . . . you will find that you knew loss was coming. Will you trust us, this family circle into which you've been drawn – Father, Son and Holy Spirit? Will you forgive us, even without understanding it all? Will you forgive me, your heavenly Father? It's vital. You must do it or you and your whole family will come under a shadow of misery that could last for decades.

Helen represents the very best of you. She shows all hell and all heaven just what has been accomplished in the last fifteen years. Even while you grieve, rejoice in her triumph. Many people say they are ready to die for their children. Helen actually did it. She is one of the jewels of eternity. Remember, it's not just about you. Be angry with me, Billy, but don't sin by holding on to it. Your children need William, the true conqueror. Remember him? I am your Rock and your Fortress. It's time to make a stand. Show Tom what heroes are made of. I'm still your proud and ever-loving Dad and I know you can do it!

Your eternal Father,

GOD

AUGUST 30th

Dear God,

I don't understand. Mum has been so cruelly snatched from us just as everything was coming good for us as a family again. And now it feels like we're losing Dad. Since Mum died he's just hit the bottle and spends his days so out of it, he's either asleep or talking gibberish. Annabel has been doing her best to look after little Liberty, who keeps asking, 'Where Mummy? Where Mummy? Mummy home soon?' It is beyond awful.

I can't believe it happened so quickly, so unexpectedly – Mum just pushing Liberty in the buggy and just about to cross the pedestrian crossing, when this Peugeot 205 came careering round the corner on two wheels. She had just enough time to push Liberty out of the way before the car smashed into her. She died instantly. Turns out it was someone from my old school who'd just passed his test. He wasn't wearing a seat belt and was flung through the windscreen and died instantly – severed his carotid artery. Where do we go from here? I don't know – but with Dad permanently wrecked I'm doing my best to step up and run the home. We are devastated and I have no idea what is going to happen. Funeral next week and Sara and Thor are flying over. Victor has also said he'll come and live with us for a while. Thank God for my big brother.

The house looks like a florist's shop, and people just seem to be coming and going all the time – but Dad just sits in his chair and only moves to go to the bathroom or get himself another bottle of wine. He can't carry on like this or he will kill himself. God, in your mercy, comfort and help us. This is the hardest time.

Tom xx

SEPTEMBER 5th

Dear God,

It's me – Jack. I don't understand why Mummy died. Why did she die? Will I ever see her again. I miss her SO MUCH. My heart hurts.

Jack

Dear God,

Well, that is the hardest thing I have ever had to do. How great the pain of searing loss? Too ******** big to begin to even remotely articulate it. Over two hundred people turned up to say goodbye to Helen. Family obviously, including Sara and Thor from Canada, friends from church, the kids' schools, old university pals and even some of her old boyfriends, not to mention one or two faces from my criminal past come to pay their 'respects' (including Eddie Fast of all people – I wondered what had happened to him). And finally even a couple of coppers, kind old PC Larking and his boss Chief Inspector Don 'The Monkey' Moseley. She would have been proud to see so many people come to celebrate her gloriously loving, beautiful and tragically foreshortened life. She was carried in by Victor, Thor, Tom, Lefty and two of our best friends, Malcolm and Richard, who had been so very helpful organising things when I went to pieces in the few days directly after Helen's death. I still *am* in bits and probably shall be forever. Just a bit more articulate at the moment but it helps to get it all down on paper. All the feelings. Misgivings. Self-recrimination. Guilt. We played Eva Cassidy's song, 'Over The Rainbow', as she was carried in. It was exquisitely beautiful and excoriatingly painful all in the same breath. Tom spoke very eloquently about his mum and then Annabel and Jack sang a song about her called, 'The Fairest Flower'.

After the service we didn't hang around. I left a CD of music to play some of our favourite songs, 'Live Like You Were

Dying' by Tim McGraw, Bruce Springsteen's, 'The Rising' and The Waterboys' 'Spirit' and then the cortege drove down to our sacred place, a little church in the hills near her old home, the church where we were married. There, Helen's earthly body was laid to rest. Liberty stayed with some old friends in the town nearby but the rest of the children came and at the final point of separation they clung to Sara and Victor, while I knelt at the muddy graveside and wept. Just one person stayed with me. We clung to each other like two sailors shipwrecked and abandoned. Bonded in our grief. Soaking each other's shirts with our tears. It was Thor.

Love,

Billy

SEPTEMBER 9th

My dear son, Billy,

You *are* right. That is the hardest thing you've ever done and made harder because you walked right through pain too big even to be able to articulate it. But you walked through it. You embraced it – *sober for the occasion*. You did so well. I'm proud. I know you felt completely wrecked by the experience and weak as water. But you'll be amazed how many people watched you go through the day and walked away with more respect for Billy Fidget than they've ever had in their lives. Don't be surprised to hear from some of them. Keep on giving this tragedy to me and I'll bring more good out of it than you would believe is possible.

Of course, you are still in pieces. But let me put you straight about something; you will not be in pieces forever. You *will* be whole. Of course there will always be a part of your heart where the joy of Helen's life mingles with the pain of her loss and occasionally tears of gratitude will be mixed with grief. Don't forget, in spite of your feelings, you have no guilt in this matter. Thanks to your willingness to live in honesty with me, Helen's life was transformed. She received healing and joy that would have been impossible if you had not had the courage to walk in obedience and discipleship with Jesus.

The Enemy will accuse you. He will try to make you feel guilty. His name is Satan, and it means accuser. That's what he does. But you are a forgiven man. Walk in the grace. Self-recrimination – now that's a different issue. That's where you start to accuse yourself. But I want to stop you right there. If I have forgiven you (and my standards are rather higher than yours!), then shouldn't you forgive yourself? Don't play that game. Let Satan sink into the misery of his own emptiness and fear.

You live in the beauty of who Helen was and what she became as you walked with me. Remember, she has already begun her eternal song. Part of it is thanksgiving that she met you and you in turn introduced her to me. Her body may have gone home to where she was born, and you were married. But her spirit, the true Helen, is not there. She is everlastingly grateful for you as the link that brought her into her eternal home.

I watched while you and Thor found each other at the edge of the grave and embraced, brothers together in grief. All heaven sang praises. It is what we love to do, to take the estranged and make them friends, take enemies and make them brothers and sisters. Now you have what you always wanted and missed when you were a lad – a brother, a brother in spirit, and it's only the beginning of that. Even in the middle of the grief, do take time to celebrate the joys and the little victories, because actually they are huge.

Ever your faithful and loving Father,

GOD

Hi,

Just need to say – I'm struggling. The other night I got so obliterated I ended up wandering the streets shouting abuse and unable to walk in a straight line. I was found by PC Larking – you know, the one who was always busting me for one thing or another. Fortunately he took pity on me and took me home in the patrol car. I'd fallen over onto my face and knocked a couple of teeth out. I was a mess in more ways than one. The children were horrified. Annabel took one look at me, screamed and ran off. It was Victor who helped get me cleaned up. Tom was disgusted, and thankfully Jack and Liberty were fast asleep.

So, today is day two of trying to stay off the booze. I'm drinking lots of fruit juice and sweet tea, and eating far too much chocolate – but it seems that whatever I do there is nothing that can numb this pain. Nothing touches it. I'm not sure it will ever stop. I think I'd just rather die and be with Helen. Mind you, who would look after my family? They need me. And I need them. But I have thought about death. A lot. It seems to stalk me like a spectre at a feast of broken promises. Dr Death intrigues, beguiles and taunts my mind in my drunken half-sleep, whispering subtle deceits into my subconscious – venom cloaked in a thinly veiled guise of ill-bred sentiments and conceits.

He thinks I am on the ropes. One more sucker punch and I'll be bound for Hades. I know the dark force that plagues me: it's the same one that stole Auntie Freda away from me

181

when I was just thirteen. I was always close to her but when my mum died she lost the plot and started putting away large amounts of sherry before progressing to cheap whisky. And though in truth I didn't physically lose Auntie Freda for another twenty-seven years, she began to shrivel and slowly starved what love I had for her until I could bear no more. She wasn't much like a surrogate mum, since she could not live with her own pain or, it seems, looking after me. So she just kept looking for the answer to her loss in the bottom of a glass. Where, of course, lay even more heartache. So one day I cut the umbilical cord of emotional blackmail, broken promises, depressing allegations and dark matter. In fact, it was easier than I thought. But just six months later she was dead. A combination of liver failure and alcoholic dementia. She rotted away in a hospital bed. I always swore I would not go that way. But one slow painful day at a time I feel like I could be going down that path. I know I must fight, tell myself I'm going to make it. But oh, my heart aches.

Billy

SEPTEMBER 21st

Billy,

Nice to hear from you! It's been a few days. You're right, aren't you 'lucky' that you were found by the one copper who always liked you in spite of the fact you were a rogue, and he took you home – funny that, isn't it?

I saw you. You were a mess and not just physically. I have a question, a simple question really. Do you want Annabel to keep seeing you the way she did that night? Or Tom – do you want to see that look of disgust on his face in the future? I know you don't. So let their faces sit in your memory, reinforcing the determination you have right now not to go back that way.

So, here's my challenge – don't focus on *not* being an alcohol abuser, or that will become your focus and determine your identity. Instead, fix your ambition on being what I have created you to be – a hero. You can't numb the pain. So roll with it. When you love someone as amazing as Helen, the depth of the pain reveals the scale of the loss. Your loss has been massive. So, the pain is huge – embrace it. It's the price of your kind of love. Wasn't she worth it? Look at your family. Doesn't each one of the children remind you of her one way or another? Start to write it down. You'll be amazed and a little tiny shaft of light will begin to fill the grief with joy.

As for the one you call 'Dr Death', he has dogged you since you were thirteen and the day your mum died of cancer. The demonic spirit of death is too powerful for you and if you try to fight him, you will increasingly step onto his territory. So instead, grab hold of life, embrace life with all the passion that you possess. Determine that you are going to live in such a way as to truly be the other half of Helen. She died a hero. I'm challenging you to live as one. I know you were close to your mother's sister. But you don't have to follow her path. She took up heavy drinking when your mother died. You have a choice. Are you going to follow your Auntie Freda and let Helen's death lead you into a ghastly debilitating exit that robs your children of their father? Or are you going to stand up and be the man I've called you to be? You've made the choice before. It's time to confirm it and move forward. You're my son and I know you can do it.

Your ever-loving Father in deepest and highest heaven,

GOD

SEPTEMBER 30th

Hello Billy,

This will be a bit of a shock. It's Eddie – Eddie Fast. I know you saw me at the funeral. I didn't want you to get the wrong idea. I wasn't there to take the piss. I was there to pay respects. Your Helen was not just a looker, she was a genuine 24-carat lady. Looking back, I'm ashamed I put her through what I did. You were a right scumbag and were asking for it – all right? But I shouldn't have done what I did. Tell you the truth, it's been haunting me ever since. I know I was out of order. It was like I couldn't stop myself. Thing is, I can't forget it. Maybe I'm getting religion! That'll be a turn-up for the books, won't it? So, here's the thing, can you put aside the past and let bygones be bygones? I need help and I've got nobody else to turn to, nobody who will listen and not give me grief. Course, if you wanna tell me to naff off, I'll understand. But do me a favour, this thing in my head's driving me mad and I've got nobody else.

See ya! (I hope).

Eddie

OCTOBER 1st

Billy,

I thought I'd drop you a note after the funeral. 'The Monkey' and I were impressed. You pulled yourself together and you made it through that service. I don't know how you did it. Course, the lads down the station remember the Billy Fidget of fifteen years ago, always sailing close to the wind and often stepping over the line. But you were smart. It was always difficult to prove anything. But we knew what you were like. Then we heard that you had faced down Eddie Fast, been nailed to one of your own motors as far as I could work out. You turned your life around, you and Helen on track, your kids growing up a credit to you. Even Tom's turned himself around after that little escapade. But, to be honest, when Helen died like she did (I wish the little bastard that did it had lived. I'd love to have got my hands on him!), we all thought you'd totally fall apart.

To be honest, I wasn't particularly surprised when I found you in the road off your face. But 'The Monkey' and me were saying at the funeral that you look like you'd turned a corner, like somebody had put high-tensile steel in your backbone. Basically, we looked at you and we just wanted to say 'Respect!' Mind you, if I ever find you off your face in the middle of the road again, I'll run you in! But I don't think that'll be necessary somehow. If you ever fancy a drink, or maybe a coffee, let me know.

All the best,

Trevor Larkin

OCTOBER 3rd

Dear Mr Fidget,

I just wanted to say a big thank you for letting me be one of the people who carried in the coffin for your wife. Mrs Fidget was one of the most lovely people I've ever met in my life. I never had a mum, not that I remember much of anyway. She was like the mum I never had. I could see where Tom got it from – and there must be some from you, of course. But it was something special. I want you to know that doing it that day, carrying the coffin, was one of the biggest honours of my life. In fact, I know it was the biggest. Nobody's ever trusted me with anything like that before, and you did.

I'm still trying to walk with Jesus every day. I get things wrong, you won't be surprised to know. But between him and Tom they seem to manage to pick me up every time. I don't know whether I'll ever wear one of them dog collars, but I do know this – I just want to let other people know about Jesus. I'm still not sure how that's gonna work out. But I know it'll be OK. I'm telling you this because I want you to know it's all down to you, Mrs Fidget and Tom. Your family's had such an effect on my life, I can't tell you. All I can say is a big THANK YOU. I know you're going through something terrible at the moment. If you were like me, you'd wanna give in. What I wanna say is – she wouldn't want you to. I hope that's OK. Thanks, Mr Fidget.

Yours,

Lefty

OCTOBER 5th

Dear God,

Well, what an extraordinary few weeks. I and the family have all received so much love and support. Some incredibly beautiful letters and the things people wrote in the 'Book of Condolence', stuff like, 'You were our bright shining star,' and 'Your smile lit up any room you walked into.' But my favourite one is this: 'I'm not sure where you've gone. I just know they're going to have a great time when you walk in and I just want to be there with you.' Now, though, the phone has stopped ringing, the letters have stopped coming and the long slow grind back to some kind of normality begins.

It is great having Victor here – we often sit up late into the night talking. He's such a tender-hearted young man. I hope he finds his Helen someday. He does go on about his mum, though, with this Conan chap. He says they're a complete mismatch. In actual fact, Sara has written and said she's coming over for a couple of weeks at the end of next month, and could she stay? Annabel and I have been doing the bulk of looking after Liberty, and Annabel's school work has been suffering, so it will good to have a woman about the house. Lib, as we call her, hasn't really taken it all in. She's intuitive enough to know things are not as they should be but can't as yet work out why. Jack is really hurting and keeps saying, 'Why us? Why our mum?' My answers feel inadequate in the context we find ourselves in. Tom is being stoic and reading his Bible a lot. I worry that he has started to isolate himself a little, though. At least his mate Lefty drags him out at least once a week for a pizza. He's a great friend for him to have. What else can I say, God, except that I never felt life could be this hard. The amount of courage I have to find just to get out of bed in the morning and not lie there waiting for death is overwhelming. If it wasn't for the children I would give up. But I can't. They've lost Mum. They don't need to lose Dad as well – but I still struggle with the drink.

Love

Billy

PS By the way, Eddie Fast wrote to me. He seems to have had some kind of weird spiritual experience. I didn't reply but as far as he's concerned he can shove it where the sun doesn't shine. My knee still twinges on cold winter days and frankly I don't give a damn for that scumbag after what he put my family through. Strange, though. He seemed to be aware of that. Said he really liked Helen and what he did has been haunting him ever since. Ha! Eddie Fast getting a run down Redemption Road? Pull the other one, it plays 'Jingle Bells!'

OCTOBER 6th

Dear Billy,

Absolutely correct. This is the time when the hard yards start. The pain of loss hasn't begun to recede but people think you should be 'getting over it by now'. I'm glad you enjoy the times you sit up late talking with Victor. You're right, he is a tender-hearted young man. I wonder what he would think of his father if he knew how he had responded to Eddie Fast? Would he say, 'Right on, Dad!' or would he just look at you with disappointment on his face?

My Son once told his disciples a story. It became known as 'The Prodigal Son' and a great favourite. However, people still often take it the wrong way, just as they did when Jesus first told it. A young man claims his fortune and wastes the lot on prostitutes and wild parties. He winds up in a real mess and cries out to God (sound familiar?). He goes home, tells his father he has been a complete idiot. He wants to say, 'I don't deserve to be your son anymore. Just give me a job.' He doesn't get that far. His father wraps his arms around him, welcomes him home and gives him the keys to the house all over again. (I hope that rings bells too.) Then when they get home and begin to celebrate with a wonderful party, loads of dancing and drinking and feasting, his older brother comes home. He loses it with his father and says, 'All these years I've slaved for you. You never gave me anything. Now this waster comes home and you treat him as if he's your favourite son.'

I'm sure you've heard this story. Here's my question – which one are you? I bet when you first heard it, you identified with the foolish young man who needed rescuing. What amazes me is how often and how easily Prodigal Sons who come home promptly turn into Older Brothers. Remember that stuff about 'Love your enemies, do good to those who hate you, bless those who curse you, pray for those who treat you badly'? Jesus didn't just teach it – he lived it.

You're not just a child of our house, Billy. You're a disciple, an apprentice in my workshop and I'm the Master Craftsman. When you first wrote to us, I looked beneath all the mess of your screwed-up life. I looked beneath the filth and the muck and I saw something amazing, a diamond shining. I was right; you've begun to shine just like that. Now Eddie Fast is turning towards the Father's house and he wants help from you. If you still can't see it, why don't you ask Victor what you should do? Sometimes children are the ones who lead us best.

Your loving father,

GOD

OCTOBER 8th

My son,

Thanks so much for your letter. I know some days can be good and others seem impossibly bleak. Remember you will have a visitor soon – when Sara comes, she's not just arriving to take care of Annabel. She is a woman of God and you may find she has things to say which will speak very deeply to you. The most important thing you can do for the children apart from loving them is to pray for them. When Annabel starts painting again, there will be a new depth to her canvasses. I know young Jack is hurting. I will stay close to him. As far as Tom is concerned, when you fell apart after the death of Helen, so much weight descended on him, even the weight of holding up his father. So he needs some solitude now in order to come closer to me and regain his equilibrium. That's OK.

As for you, my son, I know life is hard at the moment. But it will not always be like this. You're right; your children shouldn't lose Dad as well as Mum. But what kind of dad are you going to be? A dad who can even reach out to someone like Eddie Fast? Or a dad who makes allowances for himself but not for others? I repeat what I said before. The challenge before you is to stop wallowing in your self-pity and commit yourself to living as a hero. You made that choice once before. It truly is time to pick up that decision and run through it again. Part of that is to lift your eyes and seek 'the impossible dream'. I said to you once, 'Part of your destiny is to take the thing you're passionate about, surrender it to me and let it become something that serves my kingdom.' Let me know what you think. Lift your gaze away from all the problems and your own tiredness and seek the vision. You're my son and I know that you can do it.

Always your loving heavenly Dad,

GOD

OCTOBER 20th

Dear God,

Thank you as always for your wisdom. It will be great having Sara around and I feel a lot better now. Regarding Eddie Fast, of course I know you are the source of all forgiveness. But as Billy Fidget I'm struggling to step up to the plate. I know dealing with him is one of the last strongholds of the 'old' Billy that I have to deal with. Just give me a break, will you? Surely you understand these things take time. I'm just not ready yet. It's alright for you in heaven and all that! But it's really hard down here!

Billy

OCTOBER 21st

Hello Billy,

I got your latest. Maybe you're forgetting, I've already paid the price for everything Eddie has ever done, as well as for everyone else in the world. As far as I'm concerned, he's forgiven. But he has to accept that. When it comes to me being the source of all forgiveness, that's true. That's why it's never impossible to forgive. I have already forgiven and people can draw the spirit of forgiveness from me if they are willing to do it. Remember what you saw in the garage when Eddie Fast shattered your knee? Hands that were rough, but gentle, with huge nails being hammered through them. My Son's face twisted and his body writhing in agony. You saw that. I know you remember it.

Billy, what you've got to understand is that forgiveness *is* tough. I know your emotions are raw at the moment and Eddie turning up at Helen's funeral felt like an affront to you. But that didn't cause the rage. It just exposed it. You've seen it on one of your fancy cars, a bit of a knock and suddenly paintwork that looked immaculate flakes off to reveal a load of packing underneath, a real duff job. You know there's nothing to be done in that situation. You've got to strip the whole thing. You've got to take it back to the original bodywork, and get it back into shape. You know it's going to be worth it because the car's worth something – but only if the job is done right.

That's the way it is with you. Eddie being at the funeral chipped the veneer off, exposing the simmering rage underneath. That's why this *is* the time to deal with it. One of the last bastions of the 'old' Billy has to be surrendered to me so that I can take it over and make it new. If not now, then when? This is the right moment. Finally, no, I can't forgive Eddie Fast for his offence against you. I can forgive him for every action which wounded me, including the way he treated you. But only *you* can forgive the offence against you. You have to do it before you see him face to face. I realise it might take time but you must take control, make up your mind and forgive. My Son did it when they were hammering nails into him. Why not ask him how to do it?

Always your

Dad x

OCTOBER 26th

OK, Jesus,

Father God says you can show me how to forgive Eddie Fast. How? Was it easier for you because you are his Son? My mum was hardly the Virgin Mary and my dad wasn't God Almighty – though sometimes he acted as though he thought he was! So how do I do what you did? Forgive someone who's caused me unbearable pain? Sometimes I wish you would come down from the cross, take my hand and show me . . . help me – please.

Billy

OCTOBER 26th

Billy, my brother,

I think you're really asking me whether I actually became human – or was I cheating, looking like a human being on the outside but made of steel on the inside. Like Superman, maybe? The answer is that I really did become as human as you. I had to leave behind everything in myself as eternal Son of God that didn't fit with being an ordinary human being. Everything except the heart and love of God and my vital connection with Father and the Holy Spirit. So there were no super powers – just me.

It had to be that way. How else could I become truly your brother? Do I know how hard it is to forgive someone who is causing me unbearable pain? Yes, I do. How did I do it? I determined that I would stay in the love of the heavenly Father no matter what was thrown at me. I let him show me the life, loneliness, pain and cruelty of the man hammering in the nails. I saw the hardness in his face. I chose my response – love. 'What he's doing will not control me. I won't let his actions fill me with bitterness, hatred and rage. I'm taking charge. I AM going to forgive.' I held that until every fibre of my being agreed. That's how *you* do it, Billy. It's an act of authority.

You haven't realised it yet, but when I was on the cross you were already in my heart! Take hold of that. Stand with me and begin to take charge. Don't try it on your own. Use my name. Speak it out: 'In Jesus' name, I forgive Eddie Fast.' As long as you hate him because of what he did, his evil is still controlling you. But when you refuse to hate him and decide to forgive, right then he loses all power over you and you are in charge. You fear you will be humiliated if you forgive him. But the opposite is true. Forgiveness is quite simply one of the most powerful forces in the Universe. Take courage and seize this moment. Give it a go. You're my brother and I know you can. I'm waiting. The Father is waiting. All heaven is waiting.

Your everlasting friend and brother,

Jesus

PS Don't let the enemy tell you I don't understand. Remember me in Gethsemane. Praying under the olive trees, I broke the chains. Now you've joined me, I believe you will conquer the bitterness. Your Captain and King, Jesus.

OCTOBER 31st

Eddie,

I don't know what the hell you want from me. I walk with a limp thanks to you. But I've managed to change my life so maybe, just maybe, you could change yours. Meet me in the Bouzy Rouge Café tomorrow night at 7pm. And come alone. No funny business.

Billy

OCTOBER 31st

All right God!

Just so you know.

I've written to that swine Eddie Fast and I'm seeing him tomorrow night. Are you happy now?

Billy

My son,

It's good to do the right thing. But why assume I would be happy with grudging, resentful obedience? I'm Dad, not a dictator. There's no point in you seeing him unless you let go of all of that. Hang on to the hatred, and bitterness will form the lens through which you see Eddie. So you'll never see the real guy – the one I love because I see beneath the surface. You're just about the only person who can help him. Will you?

Love as always. Your heavenly Dad,

GOD

NOVEMBER 2nd

Dear God,

I met with him. Eddie, that is. And yes, I did go with a hard heart and ice in my veins, but the man I encountered was not the Eddie of old. He still had a veneer . . . if you know what I mean. After all, old habits die hard don't they? However, his words were softly spoken and he thanked me for making time to see him. It was a pretty strange experience, a bit like looking into a mirror from a few years ago. A visit from the ghost of Christmas past. He told me that he'd had an 'encounter with goodness' that had been so powerful he had been forced to re-examine his life in the light of it. He did not expand on how this goodness manifested itself but he did say that it was time to 'right wrongs' and 'own up'.

He looked embarrassed when I first walked in. The weather was damp and my knee was playing me up a bit. He kept staring at it and biting his lip. After a while he said, 'Look, I know what I did to yer was completely wrong. I was, as you know, very ******* angry. You took my wife, she did stuff to you I only get to dream of and you had her in the back of one of your dodgy motors. I wanted to kill you. Actually, I'd already paid someone to do it and then had second thoughts – I was going to top you myself. Thing is, when I saw how you gave your life for your son, I couldn't do it. I couldn't deprive your lad of a father. You see, I never had a dad. So I gave you something to help you think twice before shagging somebody else's missus again. Still, what happened that day has haunted me ever since.

204

Yes it was rough justice, but it was the way we did things then.'

And as the words came tumbling out – so did poor old Eddie's heart. He'd been in a care home. Never knew his mum or dad and was fostered around so many homes and families he can't remember how many. He grew up angry and bitter. A lot like me. Except he started off as a petty criminal, 'watching people's cars' and intimidating the local newsagent because his skin was not the same colour. After a while he moved up in the world and began thieving professionally. Small businesses at first, like the local corner shop, before putting a proper firm together and graduating to corporations and banks.

He became the Don Corleone of Essex, if you like. He was smart, though, which is why he kept up a 'respectable' commodities business in Mayfair and never got caught. Then one night, on a stag do for his mate Ricky in Romford, he saw this girl and fell in love. It was Lola. He'd never been in love before. Poor sod didn't know his arse from his elbow. Totally smitten. He was, and I think still is, head over heels with her. And what did I do at the time? Gave her the old silver-tongued routine and had her all over bandy in the back of that old Aston Martin of mine. If I'd have been him, I'd have ordered a hit on me as well. Anyway, here's the thing . . . he starts to say, 'I had to see you. Had to say sorry for the pain I caused your family and for mashing up your knee.' And as he says this . . . he starts to cry. Yep, that's right. Big tough, hard-as-nails Eddie Fast is in front of me – a huge sloppy mess of salty tears and snot. And he says, 'I can't live with myself. Please, please forgive me.' Until that point I'd kept looking over his shoulder for his henchmen or for the wind-up and that's when the penny finally drops. Eddie Fast is being 100% full-on drop-dead for real. And that's when I do a runner.

Sorry, God.

Billy

NOVEMBER 5th

Billy, my son,

So much for wisdom coming with experience and age! You've reverted to the idiot of old. Now what will you do? You took no notice of what I said to you. You went with bitterness, hatred and a hard heart. So when Eddie cracked open in a way he has never done to anybody else, you couldn't cope, because if you had stayed one more moment you would have wept with him and you just couldn't do it.

How are you enjoying your diet of un-forgiveness? Remember what I said to you years ago? Un-forgiveness is like drinking poison and waiting for the other bloke to die. I know you can be stubborn, but you might as well save yourself a whole lot of grief. You're going to have to call him, apologise and meet him again. You know that. I know that. Let me know when you're ready. Don't take too long. It'll only make it more difficult.

While you're where you are, take a moment to think about the grace that has been shown to you. Not just by me, your heavenly Father, or even by your heavenly Brother, Jesus. Remember Haakon – he knew just what a struggle this was. I won't ask you what you think Helen would say. You know that only too well. Let me know when you're ready to act. I love you my dear son.

Your Father in highest and deepest heaven,

GOD

NOVEMBER 6th

Voicemail

Billy: *Eddie, it's Billy here. Sorry for doing a runner. Thank you for your honesty. Never thought I'd say that to you! Anyway, if you fancy another meet I promise I won't bottle it this time.*

NOVEMBER 7th

Voicemail

Eddie: *All right, Billy. We all get spooked now and again. Thinkin' about it I probably freaked you out a bit. Meet me in the Laughing Dog tomorrow night at six. No hard feelings . . .*

NOVEMBER 8th

Billy, my son,

Well done! It didn't take you long to come to your senses and you're going to sleep a whole lot better tonight because you called him. Don't be scared of his story and the way it echoes your own. You've got lots in common and you're going to get some surprises when you see him tomorrow night. You really are just about the only person who could help him in this way. You're perfect for the job. I'm really looking forward to seeing what's going to happen.

Your loving and proud heavenly Dad,

GOD

NOVEMBER 9th

Oh God,

I'm on my way out to see Eddie. I know I said I wouldn't bottle it, but wow – am I scared! Just so you know, I wouldn't dare go if you hadn't promised to go with me. I'll let you know what happens.

Billy

NOVEMBER 10th

Dear God,

So I met Eddie at the pub last night. He made quite a sight, sitting there, drinking a large glass of claret, in his tweed suit. 'Hello Billy,' he smiled, 'have you 'eard what it says in that book you like so much, to forgive people for what they've done to us? Apparently if we *really* forgive and let go then God will forgive us for all the crap we've done, all our crimes and misdemeanours. That's got to be a relief hasn't it?'

I looked at my shoes and then he said, 'Do you wanna drink?' I nodded mutely and then as he poured the claret into my glass, something powerful stirred in my chest and my breathing became very rapid and I felt as if I was going to be violently sick. And in a way I was. Sick of the enmity that un-forgiveness causes. Sick of the bile that forms in my head and comes out as four-letter words when I'm alone behind the wheel of my car and no one else can hear me.

Then my words came out in one long torrent but this time I heard myself say, 'Eddie, I am so sorry for using your wife and defiling your marriage. I deserved to die for what I did. And the limp you gave me . . . well, yes, it hurt like hell for about a year afterwards and I still get twinges. But they remind me to stay on the straight and narrow. So don't feel bad. I have been forgiven many times and so I must forgive you and in doing so ask for your forgiveness for sleeping with Lola.' Not my best speech ever, but a true one.

He downed his claret, looked me firmly in the eye, paused and then said, 'Thank you. By the way . . . I forgive you too.

You see, Billy, I realised through what happened just how lonely Lola was and how I'd completely taken her for granted. I won't say it's been easy. It hasn't. But we're back together now and stronger than we were then.'

Then he got up quickly, said, 'Bless yer, Billy' and left via the back door. It is taking me a while to process all of this, but I think it's good.

Billy x

NOVEMBER 10th

Well my son,

Didn't I tell you that you were in for some surprises? Eddie sitting there with a large glass of claret was not exactly a huge surprise. But he's obviously more than a little curious about the Bible as well. Then to have him smiling and talking to you about real forgiveness. I suppose the biggest surprise for you was the way his words and his smile undermined your bitterness and released you from your anger.

The truth is there are moments when all the muck inside just has to come out. Believe it or not, Eddie Fast – yes, Eddie Fast himself – was acting towards you as a kind of priest, releasing you from the burden of the past. Come on, admit it, I am a God of surprises aren't I? I'm not even going to make a bet. I *know* you never expected that.

You're right, it's all good. But the question is, what will you do with that now? As I said before, at the moment you're the only person who can help Eddie move forward. How are you going to do that? You know now he wasn't kidding. When he said, 'Bless yer Billy,' he wasn't joking. So what do you think Haakon would do? What a moment. What an opportunity to move forward and leave behind all sorts of stuff that has sat inside you for so long, a chance to grasp the destiny I have for you. You don't yet know what my plans are, but I assure you they are good. You wouldn't believe how good!

These last twenty-four hours have been pivotal, like a hinge on a huge door. As the door swings open, grab the chance and walk through it. Let me know what you plan to do. Remember this – you live under my smile. I really am your proud Dad.

Your Father in deepest heaven,

GOD

NOVEMBER 11th

Dear God,

It's kind of cool but also a little annoying that you're always right! I'm glad that through you I eventually had the moral courage and also the example to follow in Haakon, to do the right thing and meet with Eddie. Thinking about it, he had a light in his eyes and purpose in his step that I'd not seen before. I kept in mind what Jesus wrote to me. It really helped. I know it's a bit of a journey. Tell him, 'Thanks!'

Had a bit of a chat on the phone with Sara – just a couple of weeks now until we see her. Practical stuff mostly, but I've missed her. I'm really looking forward to seeing how she is, and finding out just what's been going on with this chap Conan and how she is managing her own grief over Haakon, and now Helen.

The kids seem to be bearing up OK at the moment. I think the knowledge that Sara is on the way has been something that they too have been looking forward to as a beacon of hope on the horizon. I wonder if she knows how much she means to us all?

Am pretty tired at the moment as Liberty is not sleeping through the night, and tends to wake around 2am for an hour and then is up with the lark at six o'clock. Do you know that if you look up the word 'knackered' in any dictionary that you'll find my name written by it as the definition? Not really . . . still, I hope it made you smile . . . Can you please have a word with your celestial pals and make sure I get a least one night's decent kip before Sara arrives?

Thanks, God.

Love,

Billy x

PS I've invited Eddie to join us for church in two weeks' time on Sunday and then for lunch afterwards . . . should be interesting.

NOVEMBER 20th

Hello God,

Eddie here. I've been invited to church with Billy and all the Fidgets and back for lunch after. I got no idea how they're going to react to me, especially his kids – and Tom in particular – but I guess I'll just have to find out . . . I'll be in touch. By the way, what's church like?

Eddie

NOVEMBER 21st

Eddie – Hi!

Well, that'll be a turn-up for the books, won't it? Eddie Fast going to church! But you've said yes now, so I guess you'll have to do it. Even if only because if you don't, they'll think you've chickened out! Don't forget that since the last time you saw Tom, I've come into the equation. You might just find that changes things. When it comes to church, I have to tell you that sadly a lot of them are places even I find hard to stomach. But the one they are going to take you to is a good one. I think you'll enjoy it.

Yours,

GOD

NOVEMBER 26th

Hi God,

Well, that has to be one of the most surreal experiences of my life. Meeting Eddie Fast in our parish church and then having him come back home for lunch. I was terrified at first – but the funny thing was . . . so was he. He started by apologising to us all for hurting Dad, and then said how sorry he was about Mum and that he wanted to do anything he could to help us. Finally he said, 'I think I am beginning to know what real love is. And maybe this church stuff does make sense after all.' It was amazing. Dad got up – went over to Eddie and hugged him. They were laughing and crying at the same time, jumping up and down with excitement. Like they'd scored the winning goal in extra time in the FA Cup Final. It was infectious. We all started to giggle, and then laugh out loud, until eventually we just sat there crashed out, drinking tea in a rosy-coloured silence.

Will write again soon.

Love,

Tom x

NOVEMBER 28th

Hello Tom,

Thanks for yours. It was great to hear from you. I love your story about Eddie Fast coming to church, then you lot having him back home for lunch. You're right, he *was* terrified – of going to church and even more terrified of coming back to meet you as a family, especially you, Tom. But you did well. I know your mother's death put things on hold for a bit, but I think it's time for you to go up to college to train as a minister in the church. Remember – you are already in training as a minister of God. When they ordain you they will be recognising my call upon you, not creating it. First of all you are my son and my servant. It won't all be easy. Never forget this day, because Dad and Eddie weeping and laughing together is reality.

A lot of the stuff you'll be talking about will be so theoretical and far away from reality, it will seem like fantasy. But this is truth – two broken men hugging each other because in Jesus they've discovered forgiveness, freedom from the past, new life and a new ability to love old enemies. This is the good news. It's the only thing that can change your world. No wonder it released such laughter and joy in the family that you were reduced together to joy-filled silence. Treasure it, because that is the reality of heaven breaking through into your world.

Great to hear from you. I look forward to your next.

Your loving Father in deepest and highest heaven,

GOD

Hi God,

Well, I'm 35,000 feet above your glorious planet, bound for England and the family I love. I said goodbye to Conan last night – he didn't want to come to the airport. I think he might be feeling a little jealous – but I don't know why. His parting shot was, 'Can't this guy stand on his own two feet?' It's not a complicated relationship most of the time – we go out for dinner, eat good food, drink the most delectable wines and it's fun.

I am really looking forward to seeing my family, though. It will be tough without Helen, like a jigsaw with the one final piece missing . . . except Helen isn't stuck down behind the sofa. She won't be coming back . . . which I think is what is driving me to England. I need to be with those I love. To smell the skin and breathe in the air of family, to laugh and cry together. Especially looking forward to seeing our son. Will keep you posted.

Love,

Sara

NOVEMBER 30th

Hello my dear daughter,

It's rather a while since you last wrote. I understand. I wasn't surprised Conan did not come to the airport. I know it's been hard losing your dad, even though it was expected. But then came the devastating blow of losing Helen. Maybe you carried on with Conan because you felt you deserved a little harmless fun, even if the relationship wasn't really going anywhere. It's time to face your grief now, though, to embrace it and receive grace for it which will enable you to truly move on.

I know you're going to enjoy being with the family. You are drawn to England by more than just a sense of something lost. Incidentally, you have no idea how much they're all looking forward to seeing you. You may find for the first time in a long time you will experience what it is to be 'home'. The kids are truly longing to see you and Victor is even more someone you can be proud of.

As ever, your loving Father,

GOD

NOVEMBER 30th

Hi God,

Sara's just gone to bed. It was an emotional reunion to say the least. I didn't realise just how much I'd missed her. The children were delighted and couldn't stop cuddling her, although the first question Victor asked was, 'How's the incredible hulk?' I think he was referring to her boyfriend. All Sara said was, 'I don't think he's very happy,' to which Victor responded, 'Good. He has no real idea how special you are.' Jet-lagged and tired, she simply nodded and said, 'That's enough now, Victor, please.' And the matter was dropped. Curious to see how we all get along when she's over here. She does seem to have brought an awful lot of stuff with her.

Will be in touch soon.

Love,

Billy

PS I gather Tom wrote to you about our lunch with Eddie. As the song says, 'You're an amazing God!'

DECEMBER 1st

Hi there Billy,

Yes, Tom did tell me about Eddie's visit to church and his lunch with your family. Well done for inviting him. You really were acting as my boy when you did that. It's my heart you see, to invite in all those who don't yet belong, no matter what they're like, what their history is or where they've come from. The lost, lonely, abused, guilty, rejected, fearful and wounded – we love welcoming new members of the family and that's just what you did. That's why you were so free on that day. I was glad to see you no longer holding back. When the two of you wept and laughed together, you released the whole family to enjoy it, to sense the truth that heaven *was* dancing around you.

It's a really good job it happened before Sara came back, as it truly released you all to welcome her in a special way. You have no idea how much good it did her to have the children hug her the way they did. She just didn't realise how isolated and alone she had become. When Haakon died, she busied herself with attending to his funeral and dealing with his estate. Then just as she was coming into some place of normality, Helen was ripped from her, leaving her horribly sore and raw inside. She was just about hanging on but when Victor came to England the grief overtook her – loneliness and even, at times, despair. To be cuddled by your children was immensely healing.

Her relationship with Victor is a little strained. But it will heal. When it comes to the luggage, even she does not really know why she brought so much. If you think about it, you will see that it reflects a sense of loss, emptiness and a deep longing for home. She needs a refuge, a time to weep and place to grieve and a refuge which will set her free to find her way home to me. It will take time, but I will be her place of healing. I will restore to her heaven's happiness and she will smile again. Give her time, space and quiet. Eventually, you will see the beauty inside begin to shine once more. When you feel puzzled, trust me. I am working out my purposes and believe me, they are good.

Your loving Dad in deepest and highest heaven,

GOD

DECEMBER 4th

Dear God,

Well, I'd forgotten just how nice it was to have a woman around the house. I came home from work to find that Sara had cooked us all dinner. I promptly burst into tears, because the last time that happened was when Helen was alive. We've tended to live on a diet of microwave meals, pasta, pizza, oven chips and the odd bit of cucumber and tomato, so it was a real treat.

Later that night, when the kids had gone to bed, we opened a second bottle of wine and she told me all about Conan. She's not happy with herself for diving deep into a relationship with him; as she puts it, 'That's not me at all. But I guess I was just so lonely wallowing around in the grief pit, and he showed me some attention and kindness, and before I knew it I'd gone a long way further down the line than I ever wanted to. I think he maybe knew that. It's not like he's a predator or something but I got the feeling he'd perhaps been here before with other vulnerable women. I guess he sees himself as a dashing white knight rescuing damsels in distress. The truth is he's more of a shabby grey. And I don't want to go back to him or Canada for that matter. I want to stay here in England.' I could tell from the look on her face that even she didn't know she was going to say any of that until it came out of her mouth!

And it was when she said that last sentence that something instantly connected in my brain and I heard myself respond, 'Well, why don't you stay with us?' So that's what's happening. For now at least, until Sara can get her head and heart sorted. Everybody's delighted except me. I mean, I'm glad – very glad to have her in our lives again . . . but there is this vacuum called Helen . . . and when I look at Sara and the way she is with all the children . . . well my heart is warmed and strained at the same time.

Write soon please.

Love,

Billy

DECEMBER 5th

Dear Billy,

Your first paragraph was very interesting. It is clear you are not a 'new man'! I told you I had some surprises for you and there are more to come. Take care of Sara, Billy. She is a daughter deeply loved in my heart. Treat her like the woman of God she is: with honour and respect. Help her to rediscover what she once knew: that despite the pain of loss, my grace is always bigger. When Jesus died, all heaven saw the blood from his side fall to the ground around the cross and it became for eternity the point of cleansing for all who dare to come and claim its power. Nothing is greater than the power of the blood of the cross. It can cleanse anyone. Let her rediscover that and you will see the shadows begin to lift.

Well done for inviting her to stay with you. It was a kind and generous act. It will give her a chance to re-orientate herself to England and to discover the right place for this phase of her life. I suspect that having her near will stir all sorts of memories about Helen. You also still need healing. But I can see it coming and the warming of your heart is part of it. I love it, Billy. I love bringing about wonderful plans for my children. Keep on trusting me and following one step at a time. It's going to be great!

Your ever-loving and eternal Father,

GOD

DECEMBER 23rd

Dear God,

Thank you for your letter. You're right, as always – I am in need of healing. I feel it deep inside me. Somehow, with Sara being here and us all here as a family, I feel like the process has started. Strange though, I look at Sara and even after all these years still find her beautiful. It's a beauty and a grace that comes from her soul – so that she's not just pretty to look at like any woman in the street but she shines. Radiates even. And she's just incredible with the children. Such an affirming, loving way with them all. She seems to know just what any one of them wants at any given point in time. It's weird but I feel that somehow there is a future for us all. Some way. Somehow.

Happy Christmas.

Love,

Billy xx

Acknowledgements

We would like to thank Ian Metcalfe and Katherine Venn for many hours spent editing and helping us to refine this book.

Do you wish this wasn't the end?
Are you hungry for more great teaching, inspiring
testimonies, ideas to challenge your faith?

Join us at www.hodderfaith.com, follow us on Twitter
or find us on Facebook to make sure you get the latest from
your favourite authors.

Including interviews, videos, articles, competitions
and opportunities to tell us just what you thought about
our latest releases.

www.hodderfaith.com

 HodderFaith

 @HodderFaith

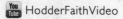 HodderFaithVideo

HODDER
WHERE FAITH IS INSPIRED